I'm In Love With Mothman

PAIGE LAVOIE

I'm In Love With Mothman
Copyright © 2022 Paige Lavoie. All rights reserved.

4 Horsemen Publications, Inc.
1497 Main St. Suite 169
Dunedin, FL 34698
4horsemenpublications.com
info@4horsemenpublications.com

Cover background and text by J. Kotick
Cover character art by Julia Korpushova
Typesetting and illustration by Niki Tantillo
Edited by SL Vargas

All rights to the work within are reserved to the author and publisher. No part of this publication may be reproduced, stored in a retrieval system, or transmitted in any form or by any means, electronic, mechanical, photocopying, recording, scanning, or otherwise, except as permitted under Section 107 or 108 of the 1976 International Copyright Act, without prior written permission except in brief quotations embodied in critical articles and reviews. Please contact either the Publisher or Author to gain permission.

This is a work of fiction. All characters, organizations, and events portrayed in this novel are either products of the author's imagination or are used fictitiously.

Library of Congress Control Number: 2022942599

Paperback ISBN-13: 978-1-64450-692-9
Hardcover ISBN-13: 978-1-64450-691-2
Audiobook ISBN-13: 978-1-64450-689-9
Ebook ISBN-13: 978-1-64450-690-5

Table of Contents

"GOODNIGHT, EVERYONE, DON'T FORGET to—" I smile into the camera lens. "—like, subscribe, follow, and remember: you have the power to do anything!" Tonight, all I want to do is disappear.

The chat has been out of control the entire livestream, and by the time my fingers press the "end" button, heavy boulders rest on my shoulders.

When Babely Beauty asked me to do a collaboration to celebrate their new skincare line, it seemed like it would be easy money. I've been a longtime brand ambassador and was eager to try their new products. How was I supposed to know it was going to launch me into the worst breakout of my life?

Though it wasn't ideal, missing an entire day of posting because of a few red spots wasn't an option.

They say the best way to keep building an audience is by being vulnerable, right? What's more vulnerable than posting an #unfiltered picture on a bad skin day?

Honest. Professional and Real.

That's what Mom always tells me to do.

"As you know, I have been OBSESSED with Babely products for years, but just like how everybody is different, so are our skins' needs. Unfortunately, their new regime and I are not compatible, but this isn't anything their soothing mask can't fix. Take care of yourself and remember you have the power to do anything! Xoxo @HoneyBeaLatte"

Then, I posted it.

Who knew the brand, and my followers, would think that I was trashing the products? The Babely team contacted me as soon as the post went live. They apologized for the reaction, sent samples in the mail for me to test out, and have been all around amazing. Unboxing the samples and doing a simple Q&A seemed like the best way to smooth things over—especially if I want to keep working with them. Unfortunately, a tagged picture of me and my Ex is apparently far more interesting than my new product haul.

@TayReads: *Did you see the new picture?*
@QueenCici: *She dyed her hair the same color as yours! It's creepy!*

Jace and I literally dated for a month—it was never serious. We would be ancient history if we didn't keep bumping into each other at industry events. The terrible thing about this whole situation is that his new girlfriend keeps getting dragged into the fabricated drama. Alice is a videogame streamer, and she seems nice as hell; the two of them look happy enough.

The unceasing ping of notifications pulls my attention back to the messages on my last post. All my photos are warm and brightly toned—a scrapbook of the most perfect moments of my life.

Even those moments aren't good enough.

@ValyGhoul34: *Honey and Jace need to get back together!*
@Pumpkin321: *Too many brand deals!*
@LouL.: *Start doing daily vlogs again!*
@Anon5: *She's only pretty because of her hair.*
@MiniMoose2: *Did you lose weight? Tell us your diet!*

A few commenters speculated that they've spotted a baby bump on one of my newer pictures. *God forbid a woman allows herself to be photographed in a baby-doll dress.* What do you say to that? I've already made at least three posts about my chronic illness. My weight goes up and down depending on my thyroid levels and the way the wind blows. I've accepted my soft curves and thick thighs; I just wish my commenters would too.

It's seriously none of their business. Just like my love life.

Every picture is called into question. People tag their friends to share their theories:

@LinaR.: *Maybe she got back with Jace? Did you see the way he was looking at her??*

@Pumpkin321: *OMG @Lina R. YES!! THEY WERE SO CUTE!!*
@MiniMoos2: *@AliceGames *side-eyes emoji**

When I comment back, they act surprised. Like somewhere between the conspiracy theories and fancams, they've forgotten that I'm a real person. The fun community that used to live in my comments section has been overrun by trolls and there's only so much blocking, deleting, and ignoring you can do. I spend hours every day answering DMs and comments trying to "tend my internet garden" as Mom always says, and it just doesn't seem to be making a difference. I thought after my @HoneyBeaLatte account hit a million followers, things would somehow feel better…

An alert chimes, and my gaze flicks down at the glowing screen in my hands. An after-hours email, just what I needed.

FWD: DEADLINE TOMORROW

Hey, Honey! Don't forget, the deadline for Babely Skincare Ad footage is tomorrow. We can't wait to see what you create.

This. This is why everyone keeps telling me to get a manager. If I miss another deadline, Babely is absolutely going to want to stop working with me. Especially after this latest "scandal"—if you can even call it that. But after the day I've had, crashing face-first into bed seems like the only way to wrap up the night.

1.

So, what if I wake up looking like a drunk raccoon?

With a heavy sigh, I haul my ring light to the bathroom and tap record on my over-heating phone. I've used their products for years, but this line is the first multi-step regime for anti-aging. Should I have been offended when they pitched it to me? Maybe, but the packaging is pretty, and the money is good even if 22 seems a little young to be doing ten steps to prevent wrinkles. At least I've worked my way past doing ads for detox tea and hair gummies. As Mom always says, "*We all start somewhere.*" Still, at a million followers, I thought I'd be past this point.

I film a little time-lapse while getting un-ready, taking special care to show each product to the camera before applying it. After the long day, it feels luxurious. My makeup melts away under my fingertips. After dipping my ring finger into the buttery-smooth moisturizer, I apply it to my skin and give the camera a thumbs up.

Easy.

Reviewing the footage in bed with a cup of tea should make work feel more relaxing, but it's not. The camera angle was somehow just a little off the entire time.

The saturation's a little off, too; it's hard to read the products' labels.

My eyes are dead.

The color is off.

My expression is tense.

Watching the footage repeatedly doesn't help, though it's a necessary part of my process. It helps to prepare myself for what the meanest comments will say.

No matter what I do, I'm continually disappointing someone—but I know I'm capable of more than this.

I'll try to film again in the morning; even if my schedule is tight, I can make it work.

I dial Mom's number. She stays up late on the weekends; knowing her, she's having a midnight snack of leftovers from a new recipe she's testing out and watching some awful murder show on Netflix.

"Hey, Honey!" The crunch of a chip punctuates her cheery greeting. "Let me pause this real fast."

Called it.

The stress of the day explodes out my lips in the form of a rant about how terrible I look on video, and how trolls and fans alike keep commenting on my body. The looming deadlines press down onto my chest, crushing me.

"I suck at this," I cry, my knees caving out from under me.

My breath suddenly feels tight, as if there's cotton candy in my lungs. I was fine a minute ago—*I was fine*—and now I feel like I'm floating, watching my body crumble from somewhere far away. And I've been calling the trolls dramatic! I'm literally sobbing while dressed in a fancy pair of silk pajamas and slippers that cost more than this month's rent.

Pathetic.

I don't know what I'm even saying anymore; my words are a senseless blubbering mess until Mom's voice pulls me back.

"Put some gratitude in your attitude!" It's been her catchphrase since I was a kid. Clamping my mouth shut, my fingers squeeze tightly around my phone.

1.

"People would kill for the opportunities you're getting—and it's never too early for anti-aging products."

"I just—don't think I can keep doing this." I twist a lock of blonde hair around my fingertips. "Re-filming this ad is going to kill me. I'm not good at this like you are."

"Of course, you are! You're just having an off day!" Mom's voice wafts through the phone's speaker. "It's in your blood. Besides, I taught you better than to post an *actually* honest review."

She's right: sugar-coating my post would have saved me a lot of trouble. I launched my own social media at sixteen, but I was a frequent "guest star" on my mom's pages before that. She's been at it since the early days of blogging. Sharing my life with strangers online has been second nature since I was in grade school. At least now I'm the one hitting the post button. It's not the first time an "off day" or unflattering angle has gotten me down. I'll snap out of it. I always do.

But how many "off days" does it take to admit that something isn't working?

"You have that big fancy event coming up, right? Maybe that will re-inspire you."

"Maybe…" Twirling around in a floofy dress does generally put me in a slightly better mood.

"Look, Honey, I know some days can be hard. I remember the kind of things people said when I started: *'Oooh, I wish I got to stay home, take pictures, and have people send me fancy-free things all the time.'* We both know it's so much more than that. But you have a successful brand. Sure, you're still growing, but don't let the trolls get to you and *don't* be afraid to hustle! You can't let imposter syndrome win. At least you don't have to deal with them on top of learning to code, right? I wish it was as easy when I got started. I had to build a whole website!" She hardly breathes between sentences, eager to remind me of how hard she had it. "This isn't all about the whole Jace thing, is it? You can't seriously be thinking about calling it quits over some boy—"

"No, Mom." Was it annoying to get so many questions about him during my livestream? Sure, yes, but things just feel … off.

What did I think she was going to tell me? That my life is hard? That I deserve a break?

God, I'm ridiculous.

"Well, thanks for listening…." I sigh, sinking low to the ground, fighting to keep the next torrent of tears at bay until after we get off the phone.

Calling her feels embarrassing enough as it is.

"That's what moms are for!"

"Love you."

"Love you too. Honey, don't stress all this small stuff, okay? Babely hired you to make a cute personal ad—they're not expecting it to be studio quality. I'm sure your video is great! Just send it in and stop worrying. We'll do coffee and talk shop next week, okay?"

That's all this is: *small stuff* I'm stressing about. A dark cloud I've crafted for myself filled with self-doubt and jitters from too much iced coffee.

Tomorrow, I'll get organized, starting with a new planner, or maybe I'll start interviewing assistants. The idea makes me bristle. If I hire someone, it's not just my happiness or paycheck on the line, but something needs to change.

1.

I flop on my bed and open my phone, clicking on my "calm" Pinterest board. I scroll through pictures of beautiful cabins in the middle of nowhere.

No cellphone.

No computer.

No commenters telling me it's "you're" *not* "your."

When I can't sleep, I crave something simple; the irony isn't lost on me that I'm staring at it on a screen inches away from my face.

Tonight, I take things a step further. I type "CABINS FOR SALE" into the search bar. I scroll through pictures until my eyes are heavy, and my heart doesn't feel like it's going to explode out of my chest.

Looking through the actual listing is much less perfect than my Pinterest board. You can tell some of the photos are taken by owners who barely know how to use a camera.

Still, there's a charm to them. What would it be like to look out the windows and see something so lush and green?

A small one-bedroom cabin catches my eye. The photos aren't perfect, but they're well-lit and clear. There are rocking chairs on the wraparound porch, and vintage-looking windows. A sill in the kitchen that looks like the perfect place to set a pie to cool down.

Quaint. Quiet. The opposite of the life I've built here.

Whoever decides they want to live in this cabin couldn't possibly be unhappy there.

For just a brief moment, I let myself imagine what it would be like to be that person.

Not that I would ever do anything that impulsive, but it is nice to dream. Or, at least, that's exactly what I tell myself as I dial the number on the listing.

"I'M NOT HAVING A BREAKDOWN."

Says the girl who buys a cabin in the middle of nowhere, sight-unseen, and ghosts every one of her social platforms.

I've been flooded with messages since my socials went dark. But nothing is as bad as the calls I keep getting from my mom.

"How could you do something so reckless?"

"If you're going to move anywhere, why not closer to home?"

"Why are you throwing away everything you've built?"

"What are people going to say?"

She spits the words as if I've done something awful, like using a cheap box-dye on my hair. Which, to be fair, I *did* also do—being a brunette sounded like a nice change. I haven't dared to share any photos.

What are they going to say?

My followers can go wild on every hate blog and Facebook group, post their conspiracy theories, and tweet to their cold hearts' content. Starting today, my goal is to be blissfully unaware of anything anyone online thinks.

Mom is convinced that moving out to the middle of nowhere is dangerous. She needs to stop watching those murder shows. I was feeling less safe back home every day. Most of my trolls were harmless; they weren't interested in hurting anything except for my ego.

But sometimes, being an influencer gets strange.

A guy once emailed me as if we'd been dating for years, and he was disappointed I'd been showing too much skin.

Someone sent me a lock of their hair, which was enough to make me close my PO Box for good.

My mom's followers can be the worst. I didn't choose the blog life; it chose me. And having a parent who was an OG Mommy Blogger has had some severe drawbacks. Even though I am a 22-year-old adult woman, people feel like they have some sort of say in my life because they watched me grow up online. It's like having a million nosy aunts commenting on every aspect of my life. People just know things about me, and some of it wasn't even my choice to share.

Then there are the threats. Those are too scary to laugh about.

I stopped geotagging my location when visiting coffee shops and theme parks because followers would show up—and the thing is, I've been lucky because they were all great.

2.

No one who came up to say "hi" had bad intentions. It's always strange and beautiful to see what kind of impact I've had from the other side of a screen. Yes, there's an enormous amount of pressure that comes along with that, but it's an honor, a reminder that in some small way I've helped.

But if they could find me when my location was tagged, so could all the people who wanted to hurt me. Delaying all of my posts by 24 hours was the obvious choice. Even still, I'm unsettled when a stranger points a camera in my direction.

Out here that won't be an issue anymore.

Nothing in the woods is going to stalk me, no matter what my mom's anxiety is telling her.

I pack up everything that makes sense—and some things that don't. There's little room to squeeze sentiment into my suitcase, but I make it work and donate or sell almost everything else.

The cabin is in Ohio, across the bridge from West Virginia. It's a cute one-bedroom log cabin that, in pictures, looks like something out of a storybook—the perfect place to find myself again. The drive takes around 13 hours. I stop in South Carolina for the night to try to break it up. My friend Sky, whom I've followed for years, lives somewhere in the city. My thumb hovers over her name, thinking about sending her a DM. If she's free, we could meet up for a much-needed coffee.

But she might hate me in real life. It's happened before, an expectation falls flat when doused in reality.

Driving through the mountains takes every ounce of my attention. My Nissan Cube was not made for the winding roads that lead to my new home. My phone's

GPS has no idea where I am half the time. Once I get to the edge of the woods, my knuckles are white from how hard I'm gripping the steering wheel. Finally, I turn up a bumpy road and see an adorable little cabin.

The realtor perches in a rocking chair on the porch—my porch.

"Heather?" There's a friendly drawl to his accent. I hesitate. I've been @HoneyBeaLatte for so long, my given name feels strange. My hand raises in an enthusiastic wave before I extend it to meet his. There's a spark in his light blue eyes that reminds me of the way my grandpa looked when he was still alive. He wears a dark green flannel, and a baseball hat covers a shaggy mane of grey hair. He looks older than he did in all our video calls, maybe that's because his wrinkles aren't pixelated in-person.

"Hi! I'm sorry, I know I'm like totally late."

"Charles Wilson! Great to have you here." His handshake is as hearty as his smile is wide. "When you said you were driving in, I figured that might be the case." The old man taps the back of the rocker. "I hope you don't mind. I made myself comfortable."

"Totally cool! Hope you didn't have to wait too long." It's like I'm showing up late to work or an important appointment— except I'm missing the iced coffee in my hand, and I can't blame this mishap on the traffic on I-4 being like *sooo bad*.

Charles is a sweetie. He shows me around with as much gusto as an HGTV host. The cabin itself is smaller than it looked in pictures, which is fine by me. It's not like I take up all that much space. The walls are dark wood logs, and the old-timey windows look like something from a fairytale. I love that all curtains are lace, and each piece of antique furniture is draped in a doily. Dust sticks to my fingertips like a layer of powdered sugar when I make the mistake of resting my hand on the dining table.

There is *so much* cleaning to do.

I sign some paperwork while Charles tell me the history of the house. It's been vacant for quite a few years and was mostly a vacation home that no one stayed in.

"People say this part of the woods is spooky. Personally, I don't see it that way. The forest bathed in the glow of the moon is one of the most beautiful sights I've ever known." Charles says placing the keys in my hands, reality sets in.

"This is my house." The admission comes in a whisper. All of this is actually mine. I gulp, taking in the small space. It's as if my Pinterest board has become a living, breathing thing with its worn wooden floors and lace curtains.

"If you have any questions, my number is on the card." His smile reminds me of the Pillsbury doughboy. Is that awful? No, no way. Who wouldn't want a cute smile like that?

"Be good to these woods, and I'm sure that you'll be very happy here."

Okay, that's a strange way to phrase it, but connecting with nature is one of the big reasons I'm here. "Yes, absolutely!"

With the warm, yet ominous, goodbye out of the way, Charles hops in his truck and gives me one final wave.

Once I'm alone, the itch for my phone returns. I fight the overwhelming urge to post a photo of my hands holding the keys.

Cheers to new adventures, the caption would read with a stream of celebratory emojis following it.

I don't know if I'm proud of myself or horrified, but the rush of feeling is undeniable. Pushing down the urge to share this moment with my followers feels like I'm putting this moment in a precious box and keeping it locked inside of me.

Crashing onto the bed seems like a good idea until a layer of dust floats around me like a cloud upon impact. Bad idea.

Bad idea!

My body contracts around a sneeze as I roll off the bed. Hopping to my feet, I throw the sheets off the mattress in one swift motion. A power nap before unpacking was the next thing on my mental checklist—but plans change. I'm actually going to have to clean this place before melting under the covers.

The first order of business is clearing some of this dust out. Pushing open each of the old windows and letting the night air soak into the cabin makes me feel like Snow White.

"Any woodland creatures want to help me clean up in here?" I call out the window. That would have totally gotten a laugh from Mom if she was here. We haven't had a nice conversation since she found out the news.

I click on her smiling face under "frequent contacts," and the choppy cell signal springs to life with a muffled dial tone.

2.

No answer. *Huh.* Texting it is.

[Me: hi I'm here safe! The house is really cute.]
[Mom: Okay. Good.]

That's it? She must be deep in work if that's all she has time for.

[Me: are you busy?]
[Mom: not really]

Then why the heck didn't you pick up? Maybe the call didn't go through after all.

[Me: Okay, well feel free to call me. The signal out here seems a little weird.]

Nothing. Not even the typing animation.

I'm being ghosted by my own freaking mother!

I sink to the ground and feel the dust-caked floor under my fingertips.

I'll clean this place up, send her pictures of how cute it is, and then she'll totally get it.

Normally, cleaning at night is a habit I do when I'm too anxious to sleep, which has been happening more and more lately. But right now, I'm dead tired. Cleaning is the last thing on my mind. I unpack my light pink portable Crosley record player—because hello, priorities. It's hard to get into the right groove with cleaning if I don't have the right playlist. The creepy, old-timey sounds of Henry Hall play through the speaker.

As I work, I feel the cool night breeze drifting through the open windows. I'd never be able to do this is Florida. The air back home always felt like stepping into a dishwasher on the steam cycle. Here, the crisp scent of pine blows through the trees—it smells like taking a sip of fresh water.

The record spins while I replace the musty sheets I'd tossed aside with the pink floral linens I brought from home; they add a soft romance to the room that's just perfect. I throw everything in the washing machine—God I'm so glad there's a washing machine—and continue to unpack my hopes and dreams.

Spinning around the table, I dust to the song's melody. When my fingertips glide along the worn windowsill, a chill starts at the base of my spine and creeps all the way up to my neck. It's a feeling I wish I didn't know so well—someone is watching me.

My eyes flick up to the woods, and I stare into the red eyes of an owl in the distance. Still, the chill doesn't subside. Maybe it's the gravity of what I've done finally hitting me or the cryptic well wishes Charles gave me before he left. Doubt builds in my chest as I force myself to stare out into the woods.

I'm going to make this work, I tell myself while closing the windows.

I need to make this work, I promise myself, locking the door.

Because if I can't be happy here, I don't know that I'll be happy anywhere.

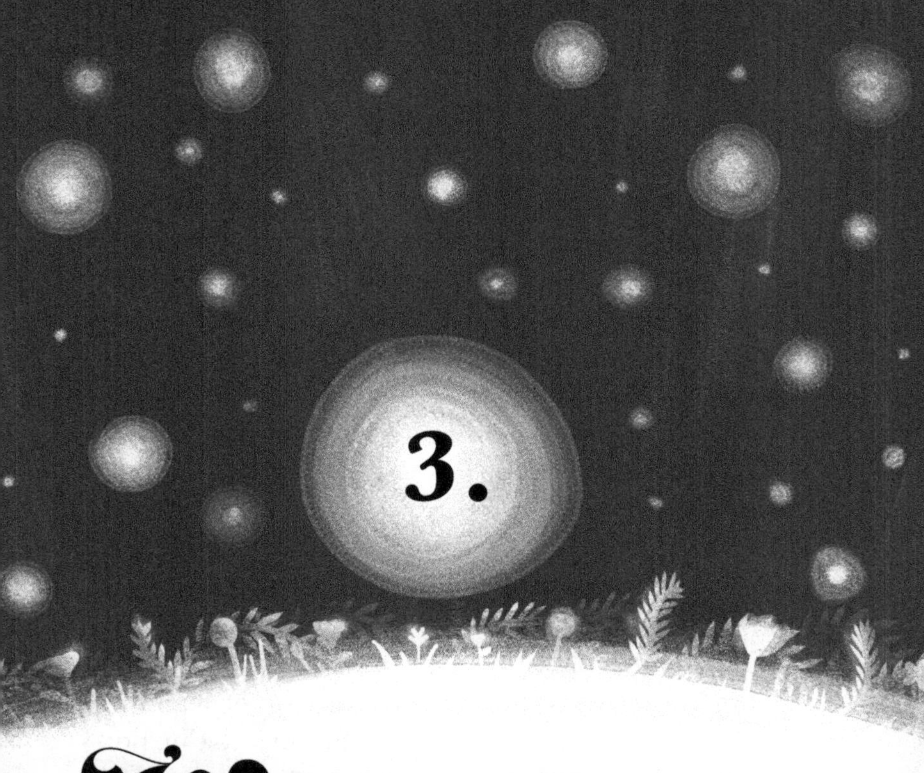

3.

WHEN YOU THINK OF LIVING IN THE middle of nowhere, you imagine silence. Every bird is louder than an indie musician trying to link you to their Soundcloud.

I'm a walking blanket cocoon as I head into the kitchen. I should have been more intentional about packing—especially after that "10 Easy Ways to Prep Your Suitcase for a Summer of Jet-setting" post that went live last year.

Ugh, what I would give for a latte delivery right now?

My frozen fingers root around in cardboard boxes until they dig out my small kettle. The eggshell color looks even brighter next to the dark wood tones of the kitchen.

The kettle *click-click-clicks* on the gas stove, while I throw back each of the curtains to drench the cabin in sunshine.

I manage to find a bag of instant matcha I got as a freebie from a new company—*made with powdered coconut milk so it's like having a café right in your pantry #gifted #sponsored*—which might have been a stretch, but the tea is sweet and with no coffee shops for miles, this is as good as it's going to get.

My burrito of blankets is even cozier with the warm mug in my hands.

#Sleepinsaturday can be every day if you try hard enough.

My brain thinks in snapshots and captions, and guilt pours through me, making every sip of tea taste bitter. Does having these thoughts mean I'm not "unplugged" enough? Why am I so bad at this?

I set the tea down and flop back on the bed, burrowing amidst the blankets.

When I wake up, my mug is cold and untouched on the nightstand. The clock reads 2pm, and the sun has shifted across my eyes.

Normally, around this time, I'd either be deep into filming or editing depending on the deadlines on my calendar.

It's strange to have nothing on my agenda.

Sleeping all day hasn't been an option in years. God, that felt like bliss. With no responsibilities to speak of, I cozy further into the blankets, missing my mattress from home.

Home.

3.

Despite having the keys, it feels like I'm in a cute cottagecore Airbnb. Shaking off the blankets, I pad across the floor to the kitchen and grab a glass of water.

The tap water tastes funny. Boiled in the form of tea, it's drinkable, but I should probably try to find a water pitcher with a filter or something.

It's not like I can just run out to Target. My phone's service is spotty, but I'm sure there was a small store on the way here. They probably have gallons of water at the very least, until I can find something better. Or they should be able to point me in the right direction. It's worth investigating, just to see what's around here.

#hermitlife can totally resume after exploring town.

The drive out of the woods is bumpy until I reach the main road. The fall leaves splay across the ground in beautiful mustard and rust shades, and crunch under my tires.

We don't have seasons like this back in Florida. I've always wanted to visit an apple orchard or pumpkin patch; I tuck the idea away for the perfect autumn day. I'll stroll around in my orange knit dress and come home to bake a fresh pie.

Daydreams of crisp leaves crunching under my boots, and crumbly pie crust on my lips entertain me until I reach my destination. It's a forest-green building with gold letters that simply reads "The General Store." There are flower boxes out front and a big dirt parking lot. Down the small street, there are a few other shops, a bar, and a restaurant.

None of them are as pretty as The General Store. The side of the building is pink with a mural of white flowers and would be an absolutely stunning #OOTD photo wall.

A bell chimes brightly when I walk through the door. Inside, it is a little rougher around the edges, with a mix of artisanal goods and staples like Wonder Bread and peanut butter. The shelves are lined with brands I haven't seen since visiting my grandpa's house as a kid.

"Hey, this is probably like totally random." My voice is shyer than usual when I approach the register. My face flushes when I meet the eyes of the girl behind the counter. Her cherry-red hair is swooped into a messy bun and she's wearing a cozy flannel. She's looking at me—no, looking at my shoes—with wide eyes.

And here I thought I was being casual. My Irregular Choice platform sneakers aren't subtle—especially since they light up with each step—but they're the only pair of sneakers I own.

Back home, they were fun and quirky. Here I think they might just be weird.

"Do you sell like a water filter thingy? Either a pitcher or something that goes on the tap?"

"Oh. No, you might have some luck at the hardware store; it's about five minutes down the road." Her voice is light and sweet. Oh no, I'm not about to get a crush on the first person I meet after moving!

I opt to buy two gallons of water just in case and peruse the aisles. There's definitely not a whole lot of packaged gluten-free options. I'm glad I packed a stash of snacks and dried goods. Still, as I move through the aisles, my arms fill with locally made soap, fresh apples, and fresh coffee beans.

3.

"Let me help you with that," a deep voice says as one of the water jugs is suddenly taken from my hands.

"Aw, you're so sweet." I don't bother to protest; my items are literally about to topple from my grasp. When I tilt my head up to find the owner of the voice, I'm met with the most apple-pie Americana face I've ever seen. He's blonde with blue eyes and a light splattering of freckles across his skin. My cheeks burn, and every possible greeting tumbles out of my head. Is everyone who lives in this town going to be impossibly cute?

"Staying in one of the vacation homes nearby?"

"Just moved here actually." The correction makes me feel a little smug. "I got just like the cutest little cabin in the middle of the woods."

His blue eyes seem to sparkle. "All by yourself?" There's something dangerous in his tone, I catch him eyeing my engagement-ring-free finger.

"Uh—" I shouldn't tell some random dude I live by myself in the middle of nowhere, but his dimpled smile disarms me.

"No, sorry I didn't mean to sound creepy. No offense, but you look like a city girl—"

"Meaning?"

"For curiosity's sake, have you ever climbed a tree?"

Okay, now I'm seriously offended. Who the heck does this guy think he is?

"I didn't realize there was some kind of test I was supposed to take—and for your information, *yes*. I can totally climb a tree." *I think.* I've never actually climbed one, but how hard could it be?

"It's just that people tend to see strange things in the woods. It's important you can take care of yourself."

He eyes the back of the store, where a large community bulletin board is posted, but it's not the flyers for guitar lessons babysitters that he's gesturing to.

In the center of the board, there's a large poster that reads: *"Monster Hunters"* with a picture of the woods and a pair of red eyes. They remind me of the owl's eyes peering at me from the trees the night before.

"Spooky," I joke, twiddling my fingers. My eye catches the cute girl behind the counter, who hangs her head, as if to say, "Not this again." Monster hunting or not, I allow Apple-Pie Face to help me with my things up to the register before he disappears into the backroom.

"You'll have to excuse my brother." Cute Girl laughs under her breath. "Chris and his friends have been looking for creatures in the woods since we were in middle school. Most of them have grown out of it by now. Though, my wife Clara swears she's seen something shadowy around the farm." She twiddles her fingers to match the witchy gesture I made to Chris earlier.

Damn.

Of course she's married. It's probably better this way, cute or not. I should not be jumping into anything with anyone right now—but I like her. If I came out here to make friends, I think I'd want to be hers.

I'll just act normal.

"Aww, you have a farm? Adorbs!" I chirp in an awkward attempt at small talk.

Some of my favorite accounts have been adorable baby barnyard animals. I literally screamed on the phone with my mom when @GideonTheGoat followed me back.

"I'm Rosie, by the way." Her smile is contagious.

"Heather," I reply. It's my name, but it still doesn't feel right when I say it out loud. I've been Honey for so many years, and now it's like neither name's shape fits in my mouth quite right.

Apple-Pie Face—*Chris*, I remind myself—swoops behind the register with a cheesy grin as if poised to strum my heartstrings. They both have the same baby-blue eyes and round bone structure. It makes sense they're related, but I don't see a ring on his finger.

Nope, nope, no. I'm not doing that.

I'm not about to move to a small town and become the bad bisexual trope from a trashy TV show. I'm *so* not allowed to have a crush on two siblings—even if they are *unreasonably attractive.*

"You should come by for dinner sometime." He is laying it on so thick. There's no question about it—he is absolutely interested.

"He lives on the property." Rosie rolls her eyes, and suddenly this doesn't feel like the first time Chris has randomly invited a girl over to her place. Mmm, apple-pie face or not, he might be a player. I should be careful. I've had enough fuckboys in my life for an eternity. "But yes, we would love to have you," Rosie adds with a smile that seems genuine.

When was the last time I went over to someone's house for a normal dinner? Even though I'm sure Chris has ulterior motives and I'm not sure of my own motives yet, I think that's totally fine.

But I didn't come here to make friends.

"Yeah, sure." I chuckle, pushing away my inner reality-show mean girl.

Luckily, small talk swallows up any clumsy attempt to exchange phone numbers. I'm happy about it really. I'm trying to set up my new life. Distractions are just going to complicate things.

I leave with my armful of groceries, waving to the hot siblings. I'm just about done loading up my car when a deep voice makes my head turn.

"Hey! Heather, right?" I turn my head and catch Chris jogging up to me in the parking lot.

"I have everything fine." Handsome or not, I don't want a literal stranger following me to my car. Still, before I have a chance to sidestep, he's standing in front of my trunk. In a practiced motion, I slip my keys between my fingers to use as a weapon.

"Here." He offers me a piece of paper. I hesitate before letting him place it in my unarmed hand. His calloused fingers brush up against my smooth skin for a moment too long.

"Rosie might not believe me, but there's something out there." Chris's eyes sparkle in the sunlight. "Call me if you need anything. I don't know what it's like where you're from, but people around here look out for each other, okay?"

"Right now, all I really need is help moving boxes." I stand tall, not willing to drop my guard—or my keys.

"I did say *anything*." He winks, and my chest flutters against my will.

Monsters in the woods. A chill creeps up my back. I brush off Chris and quickly get into my car, driving off down the unkempt roads.

Mom's been talking to me about too many of her weird murder documentaries. I shake off the awkward vibes and stop at the hardware store on the way home. I'm relieved when they have a water filter, but less so when I hear the words "city girl" whispered under someone's breath.

"Look at those shoes."

"I wonder where she's visiting from."

Everyone here is going to just think I'm on vacation. But then again, I didn't move away to fit in; I moved away to disappear.

Slamming the door of my car, I drive back home, the trees casting arm-like shadows as I turn onto the dirt road.

It's not until I pull up to my house that the feeling of being watched returns. Last night, the trees seemed to stare right into my soul. It felt daunting but somehow romantic; now I'm not so sure. On the pathway leading to my house, my light-up sneakers crunch in the leaves. Each tiny sound makes me jump.

Stupid Chris, getting in my head like this.

The only *strange thing* in the woods that doesn't belong is me. And I'm going to change that as soon as possible.

4.

I TIP MY HEAD TO LOOK UP AT THE GIANT OAK tree. Oh god, I'm going to do this.

I'm actually going to do this.

And why not? Just because I've lived in the city my entire life does not mean I can't do something simple like climb a tree. I'm dressed in one of the perfect outdoorsy outfits I curated just for a moment like this: a sweeping moss-colored skirt, peasant top, and a pair of brown boots, with my hair tied away from my face with a scarf. I always made it a point when shopping for practical clothes to never sacrifice cuteness for function and my closet is a glittering, floral, wonderland of springtime. I'm glad I brought some earth tones for occasions like this.

I hold tight to the vintage copy of *Pride and Prejudice* tucked under my arm. I can—and I *will*—have my cute tree-climbing-moment if it kills me. I place the heel of my brown ankle boot against a large piece of protruding bark to give myself a little boost. Hoisting myself up onto the first branch, my nerves begin to settle. Wow, this actually isn't that bad. By the time I've swung myself over the second branch, I start to get the hang of it. Could I use just a few ounces of upper body strength to make climbing more comfortable? Sure. But honestly, I surprise myself with every swift upward movement. I'm like really, *really*, good at this whole outdoorsy thing. By the time I've reached the top of the tree, I untuck my book from under my arm. The sun is setting, casting a golden light across the pages nicer than any reading lamp could.

I gloss over the familiar words in my book. With every second I'm taken in by the heights, my fingers jitter as if I'm overcaffeinated, but along with the nerves, there's freedom. I could do this every day if I wanted to. At the top of the tree, with the hem of my dress blowing in the breeze, I feel like a rebellious Victorian lady who refuses to bend to society's norms. The people in town can say what they want about me. I won't let their sideways glances keep me away from building the quiet life I came here for.

It's a picture-perfect moment—the kind I dreamed of creating back in my small Orlando apartment. Although, the quiet is louder than I imagined with the chirping of the squirrels and birds. Resting my back against the trunk of the tree, I'm surprised it doesn't have the support of a plush reading chair, but it's fresh and real. My feet dangle from the branches, weightless and free, while a deep and profound thought causes a lump to rise in my stomach.

How the hell am I going to get down?

Heck, I climbed up the tree.

Climbing down should be easy.

Like, *super* easy.

So, I don't understand why every time I try to move my legs, they freeze.

My phone is tucked in my bedside table. Why did I have to be so *stubborn*? Not that I would call anyone for help—it would be way too embarrassing, and who do you even call? Pretty sure the fire department getting cats out of trees is something that only happens in cartoons, and I'm a full-grown woman.

I got myself into this mess, and I can—*will*—get myself out. It's not like I'm going to slip—

Suddenly, my shoelace snags upon the rough bark of the tree, and my body falters. I wrap my arms around the base of the large branch.

The sun sets as I struggle to regain my footing. With a deep sigh, I make my decision.

I live in this tree now, and that's *fine.*

I came out here to connect with nature, so I am totally just going to hug this branch and never let go. Because if I let go…

My gaze dips to the ground, the whimsy of my skirt dancing at my heels is lost as the long fabric keeps making it impossible to get a good hold on my branch with my legs. It's no use. These boots—while cute—are doing nothing to help me get traction, the skirt is a mess, and my poor book has tumbled into the abyss below.

I can imagine the headlines now. None of the news outlets would bother to use my name or tag me. No, it would read: FLORIDA WOMAN DIES CLIMBING A TREE IN FORMAL-WEAR. I tighten my grip, using all my strength to pull my body upward. The branch bows, cracking with every feeble attempt. If I don't pull myself up to another branch, I'm going to—

Fall.

Grappling upward, my hands scrabble against leaves and twigs. Every lifeline slips through my fingers until there's nothing I can grab hold of. It's not until my body starts falling up instead of down that I realize that I'm being held around the waist by someone firm and strong.

I'm not sure how, but it feels like we're gliding through the air. The wind blows in heavy sheets across my skin. I hold tight to the body that encompasses mine, not bothering to think about how this is possible. I'm too distracted by the firm chest my head has fallen back against. I crane my neck to see their face, but even in the darkness, I can tell that something is *wrong*.

It's a prank, I decide, because it must be. That's the only reason this pair of glowing red eyes could be glowering down at me.

Chris cooked this up.

That's it.

In a small town like this, it wouldn't have been hard to figure out which cabin was recently purchased and find me.

He followed me out here and waited for the right chance pull a ridiculous prank. I have no idea how they got to me in time, and what kind of strange hang-gliding contraption he's using, but—

No, that's not right.

There are no seams to this midnight-black costume of feathers and bone. And the face! When I stare into the globe-round eyes, bile rises in my throat in place of a scream. Its strange features are a cross between an owl's and an insect's, with a beak-shaped mouth that twists downward and a body that feels the same as if a man held me tight in his arms. The impossible creature blinks, turning its attention to me. There's an unsaid tension in this moment—as if the strange thing before me can sense every ounce of my fear, and with each moment, I stare into those red unblinking eyes I feel the light drain from my very soul.

This isn't a prank. *This* is the monster.

As if sensing my fear, the creature's jaw cracks open just enough to show off a perfect row of sharp teeth. They gleam in the moonlight pristine, perfect, and ready to tear my throat out.

Think Heather. Think.

I couldn't climb down from that godforsaken tree, so I'm sure as heck not going to get away from this monster with strength alone. He's flying low to the ground—a fall that, maybe, I can survive. I can't survive *him.* Suddenly, I rear back against him and twist. Surprised, he loosens his grip just enough for me to fall a few feet, but not before he snatches my arms again. I don't let up, elbowing and scratching. My body plummets like a ragdoll dropped from a shelf, only to have him catch me by the waist with his claws. His grip is relentlessly firm, but I fight like hell until he bends to my demands.

When I finally shake myself free, I land in a rather conveniently placed pile of leaves. I don't waste any time before bursting into a sprint. I'm sure this is some kind of prank—things like *that* don't really exist. No matter how fast I run, those red eyes follow me, piercing through the darkness and right into my soul.

The screech it lets out is something from a nightmare, like dial up internet through a megaphone. The monster's eyes narrow as it lunges toward me. I guess I'd be mad too if my dinner kept running away from me. Now's probably an inconvenient time to pitch it a vegetarian lifestyle, so I try to evade its attack. It goes just about as well as the rest of the night.

I crash into the nearest oak tree.

The world is dark and fading fast as I'm scooped into a pair of strong arms. I try to fight it, but the grip is gentle, cradling me. It feels different than when the monster held me, but when I force myself to look, it's those unblinking red eyes looking down at me. My stomach twists in a knot as the creature sweeps me into the air. Against the night sky, the monster's dark wings are dotted with yellow and white spots, like the wings of a moth.

I hadn't noticed that while I was running for my life.

"So pretty." The nonsensical words tumble from my lips. The creature's back straightens as if reacting to the unexpected compliment. This is all absurd. Maybe the fall did kill me, and all of this is a strange dream. I've never been a particularly religious person. I don't believe in angels or demons, but I'm floating toward the sky and that's the only way to explain all of this. "Am I dead?" My dry throat burns with each word.

"Foolish little human." He speaks with a voice rich and deep like oak and midnight. The sound makes the small hairs on the back of my neck stand on edge. It's not a voice that should belong to a monster. "You should not have come to the forest."

5.

THE SUN IS *LITERALLY* A MILLION DAGGERS poking the surface of my eyeballs. I wish there was a discarded wine bottle at my feet. At least then I'd have some late-night bender to blame this all on. Blades of wet glass stick to every inch of exposed skin and when I comb my fingers through my hair, the strands are littered with twigs and leaves. Pulling myself to my feet makes every single bone ache with the memory of running through the woods.

I should be waking up on my nice neatly made bed, not my front porch.

A pair of black wings flutter through my memories. My stomach does such a dramatic flip that I'm glad I haven't had breakfast yet. Last night I was hunted and saved, safe and in danger—the two emotions war in my memories.

Claws on my skin.
The safety of two strong arms
And those beautiful wings.

Those red eyes seemed to make every nightmare I've ever had play at the forefront of my mind. There's no way anything from last night was real, except it was and I have the aching muscles to prove it.

Every piece of me is shaking. The last time I felt like this was after drinking an entire pot of coffee on a huge content deadline.

My fingers jitter as I unlock the door. Leaving a spare key under one of the potted plants might not have been the most cautious choice, but today, I'm glad I made it. The heavy door swings open to reveal an empty cabin—*my* empty cabin.

The red eyes burn through me. I know I've seen them before. A dream, it's all been a dream—or you know, I could be dead. That's a real possibility.

My body lies somewhere mangled in the woods, and my poor tortured soul is now damned to haunt this cabin forever. Ugh, if this is going to be my final resting place, I wish I would have had a little more time to decorate! My new curtains for the bedroom are still in the plastic packaging, for god's sake. My body doesn't pass through the wall when I accidentally bump into the doorframe, so I'll take that as a good sign.

I need to talk to another human. Chris's number was lost accidentally on purpose. He was so weird. But maybe, he was right.

I mean…

I'm pretty sure I was *flying* last night.

5.

Still, I can't bring myself to call Chris, not when the "Am I really dead?" question is still lingering. There's only one person's voice I want to hear right now.

"Hey Honey!"

"MOM!" I scream into the phone.

"What's wrong?"

"Nothing! No—no, nothing. I um, I had a weird dream." I exhale, letting myself fall onto the rough wooden floors.

"It sounded like you saw a ghost."

I thought I *was* the ghost.

"I told you. Moving all the way out there by yourself was a bad idea," she huffs. I can just picture the way her brow is furrowed in her classic "I was right" face. "You should have gotten a dog first or something."

"I'm fine!" I counter. "Like I said, it was just a weird dream."

We keep talking. I think I might still be sleeping.

"People are worried about you," she says, like it's new. Like it's something she hasn't been repeating ever since she heard about this "crazy idea." We talk until I've forgotten why I called her, and maybe that was the point.

I blink and I'm standing in the shower, washing off the dirt with water that's too hot. My skin is dry and pink by the time I turn off the tap.

I look down at my body and notice the small scrapes and cuts covering my arms and legs.

Last night *really* happened.

I don't bother to pick myself off the floor, feeling just as raw and worn as the wood beneath me. The forest monster hunted me last night, and then what?

Decided I wasn't worth eating and left me on my doorstep? I need it to make sense, but no matter how hard my brain shoves the pieces together, the puzzle is impossible. I'm going to need help.

People see strange things in the woods.

I pick up my phone again and dial the number for The General Store.

Nothing.

Before I lose my nerve, I throw myself into high-waisted jeans and a cropped cable-knit sweater and hit the road. My little car shakes with each bump on the rocky roads.

It was built for the city, and judging by last night, so was I.

"You shouldn't have come to the forest." The memory of his voice sits heavily upon my chest. How is it possible something so terrifying could sound *like that?* The creature's melodic tone still burns though me like a smokey cocktail at the back of my throat. When he spoke, it was smooth and deep, and delicious enough to want more and more—despite the consequences.

The pressure lets up when Chris comes into view, a crate filled with apples under his arm. There's a grin on his face—it's all too picture-perfect. I park, nearly toppling out of my car when my boot catches on the doorframe.

"Heather, hi!" He sets the crate down and throws an apple toward me. I try to catch it, but it clips my stomach and rolls onto the ground.

"Nice reflexes," he teases, opening the door for me. The bell above the door jangles merrily.

"Sorry, I'm not really a great catch."

"I don't know about that." His smile is all dimples and sunshine. "That apple is on the house, alright?"

I'm not sure, but I think he might be attempting to flirt with me. If I wasn't so distracted by the question on the tip of my tongue, he might have a chance too. I follow him into the store and catch Rosie's eye from behind the counter.

"Good afternoon!" She beams up at me before turning to stock the display case with what looks like an array of very delicious homemade pound cakes.

Curse this gluten intolerance.

I echo back a greeting, but my focus stays on her monster-hunting brother. How am I supposed to bring this up? "When you told me people see strange things in the woods, what did you mean?"

The light in his eyes is immediate. "Did something happen?"

"No! I mean, I think I might have seen something, but it's no big." I don't know why I'm downplaying it. Maybe it's the excitement in his eyes or how he's practically hopping over the counter to grab his jacket. "Honestly, it was probably just a dumb nightmare. He—"

"He?" Chris echoes, his eyebrow quirking in an expression that suggests disbelief.

"I mean—I don't know. I saw someone, or something, out there." I hang my head. This is all ridiculous. "Sorry for being so random. I'm sure I just had like … a super vivid dream or something. I shouldn't have—"

I finally have the emotional breakdown my mom accused me of.

I look down, focusing on the contrast between his work boots and my glittery flats. Any minute now, he's going to burst out laughing at me. There's nothing in the woods except for my vivid imagination.

"Okay."

"Okay?"

"Rosie, you can cover for me, right?" Chris spins on his heels, not waiting for an answer from his sister, which leads me to believe he does this a lot.

"Wait, where are we going?"

His strong hand envelops mine, tugging me through the store's small aisles until we are suddenly back in the parking lot.

"What are you doing?" I ask, pulling myself free of his grasp.

Chris's lips pick up in a lopsided grin. "Taking you on your first monster hunt."

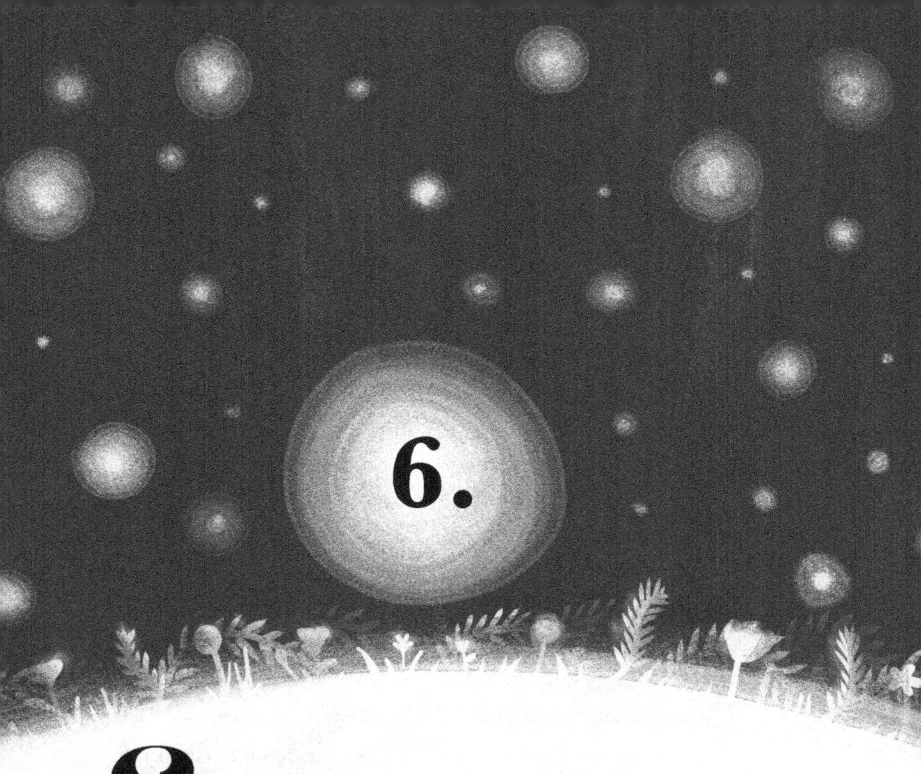

SO, MONSTER HUNTING IS JUST WANDERING around the woods with a camera. Chris begged me to stop by his place to get more of his "gear," but when I found out it included a shotgun, it was a hard no.

"I'm feeling a little nervous," I admit.

We slip under the cover of tall oak trees. I haven't told Chris the entire story. Falling out of a tree is way too embarrassing, and I'm sure I'd never hear the end of it. Still, we've been retracing my steps for the last hour, and I really wish I had been paying more attention.

"You're the one who didn't want me to bring a gun."

I don't know what to say to that. I mean, honestly, they make me uncomfortable. I don't like the idea of someone I'm with having a gun, much less using one myself.

"I'm just messing with you." He sighs. "It's broad daylight. We'll be fine as long as we're smart."

"Right," I huff.

We creep farther into the forest.

Each step we take feels like a giant risk after how the creature spoke to me last night. While the details are hazy and strange, it's like we're invading its home, though we haven't left my property. The question of how much to tell Chris nags at me. He calls this a monster hunt, but he doesn't want to kill the creature, does he? I'm scared, sure, but more than anything, I just want answers.

"Hey, gun or no gun, I'm not going to let anything bad happen to us, okay?" Chris's voice is suddenly soft, but I can't seem to relax even when he puts his arm around my shoulders in a tight squeeze.

"Have you ever seen this forest monster?" I ask. The tone of my voice accidentally shifts into something that sounds mocking. I can't help but try to lighten the mood a little. Humor can be emotional armor in the worst of times, but honestly? The more my mind wanders, the more it feels like we shouldn't be out here.

"We should keep going before we lose daylight." He avoids my question completely—which is weird. I had assumed he would want to spill every detail of every possible monster-sighting he's had. Could it be that he's hiding something?

"Right."

Each of his confident steps hit heavily alongside mine. He is tall and unwavering—it's like he's on stage for an audition. Among the trees, Chris is almost as out of place as I am. I get that he's trying to impress me, but it's surprising; he should look at home here, right?

He's nervous, and I think it's because something happened out here—something that he doesn't want to talk about.

"What exactly are we looking for?" I ask.

"Tracks, footprints, anything that looks unusual. You'll know when you see it." He walks ahead, peering around the trees. A few birds scurry away from his rough footsteps. I guess it's good to scare off any potential threats, but shouldn't he be gentler?

"It all looks pretty woodsy to me." I exhale; I swear we've passed this same set of trees at least five times.

"Come on, city girl." His arm loops around mine, pulling me along an unmarked trail. I let him lead me for a little while until we break off again to look for "clues." As the sun tips below the tree line, it's all starting to feel silly.

It was a stress dream. That's the only way to explain what happened.

Until I spot the feather clouded in shadow and lying against the roots of a tree. It looks like something that would come off a bird's wing, but it's giant. At least a foot long. I bend down, touching the soft fibers with my fingertips.

I wordlessly slip it into my purse.

"Did you find something?"

"No—my um, bracelet just slipped off," I say, hoping Chris isn't observant enough to realize I was never wearing a bracelet. Honestly, I'm not sure why I lie, but the truth tucks itself tightly in my purse next to the feather—a token so small I'm not sure why I can't bring myself to offer it to him.

Foolish little human. The memory weighs me down with each cautious step into the woods. Why do I want to hear that voice so badly again?

"If you're tired, we can take a break." Chris stops. The wind ruffles his blonde hair in front of his eyes. I'm taken by the dark spattering of freckles just barely visible upon his nose. Surprisingly boyish for someone who asked if I'd stop by his place to pick up a gun on the way here.

"Yeah—no—yeah. I'm fine." I shrug off the suggestion with a half-smile.

His hand cups around mine and leads me onward. Chris talks to me about everything. His favorite music: top hits in pop and rock, but a few indie bands in the mix that catch me off guard. How he spent last summer learning to brew his own beer. But mainly how much he misses all of the friends who've left for college.

Rosie wasn't wrong. According to Chris, back in high school, these monster hunts used to be a group activity.

"Oh, it was the best. The old gang all had their own theories, you know? It was less about catching anything. We all focused on research and discovery. There are things you just can't explain lurking in the shadows, and back then we wanted to know them all," he recounts, peppering in tales of parties in the woods and wandering through trails with his rag-tag group of friends. I find myself a little jealous. Friendships like that are hard to come by.

"Do you have a group chat or anything?" I ask, imaging they're all still in touch, and we could use all the theories they have right now.

"Not anymore." his voice is heavy with longing. "I mean, a few of us still talk sometimes, we're still *friends*, but we have some differences of opinion. Not everyone takes the threat of these monsters seriously, even if they do believe."

The far-off shift in the mood makes me question how much further I'm willing to push the conversation. Chris clearly doesn't want to divulge any more information, he's quick to change the subject, telling me about his new group of hunting buddies, ones that don't believe in "things that go bump in the night." In this new dynamic, he has something to prove—something that catching this monster would give him. Chris has been left behind by his old crew, and his new one doesn't understand this part of him. Maybe that's why he was so quick to whisk me away.

We pass a small stream that babbles with clear water and moss-covered rocks. "Moss is supposed to point you toward home, right?" I shout up to Chris, but he's too focused on our path ahead to answer.

Moss coats the rocks in the direction of the cabin. A smirk tugs at my lips. Maybe I'm not so unwanted in these woods after all.

We search for hours, snapping photos of "strange markings," fallen tree limbs, and tracks that I'm sure we made ourselves by retracing our own steps.

It's like a field trip with a bizarre teacher. Chris is passionate about this whole monster-hunting thing, but I don't know that he's very good at it.

I'm relieved when the day is finally over, and we load into my car. I'm tired and Chris is visibly discouraged. Finally, I clear my throat as I steer on to the main road. "Sorry it was a bust. I really think that flyer at the shop must have freaked me out," I say over the sound of my "chill jams" Spotify playlist.

"Hey, it's okay. It happens. You have my number if you see anything weird, alright?" He gives me that apple-pie smile again, but it doesn't quite reach his eyes. "*Anything weird* at all, okay? Don't second guess it."

"Right."

"The first rule of the Monster Hunters Club is no threat is too small to look into."

It's kind of sweet how he was willing to just drop everything and look for possible threats out here with me. Maybe I won't be as alone out here as I thought. At the very least, today I got to explore the woods behind my house with someone who'd make sure I didn't get totally lost.

"And the second rule?" I let out a small laugh, wondering if he's about to recite the entire rulebook.

"No secrets." The flat tone of his voice catches me off-guard.

"A girl has to stay mysterious," I say, trying to defuse the energy. He couldn't have noticed me stashing that feather in my bag, could he?

"I think you're plenty mysterious, Miss New Girl in Town." There's an edge to his laugh. He reaches over, letting his hand brush against my leg. "You know, people are already whispering about you."

"Great. Just what I wanted." I turn up the music, ignoring the pressure building at the base of my chest.

He gets the idea, muttering an apology and removing his hand.

A calm, peaceful life.

A calm, peaceful life.

I let the words echo through me, hoping they'll take hold.

"Why did you move all the way out here, anyway?" he asks. "No offense, but I didn't really think you'd be the wilderness type when we first met."

"Yeah, you made that pretty clear." I force out a lighthearted laugh. "I was just looking for a change of pace."

God, I sound like I'm in the witness protection program or something.

"You didn't answer my question either," I say, pulling to a stop in front of the store. "What have you actually seen in the woods?"

"Next time." He waves me away with an overconfident wink.

"Now who's the one with a secret?"

"Yeah, yeah." In the blink of an eye, his seatbelt is off and he's standing outside. He shuts the door, resting his hands on the open window. "Drive safe! There's supposed to be some rain tonight!"

I'm from Florida; it's not like *some rain* will get me down.

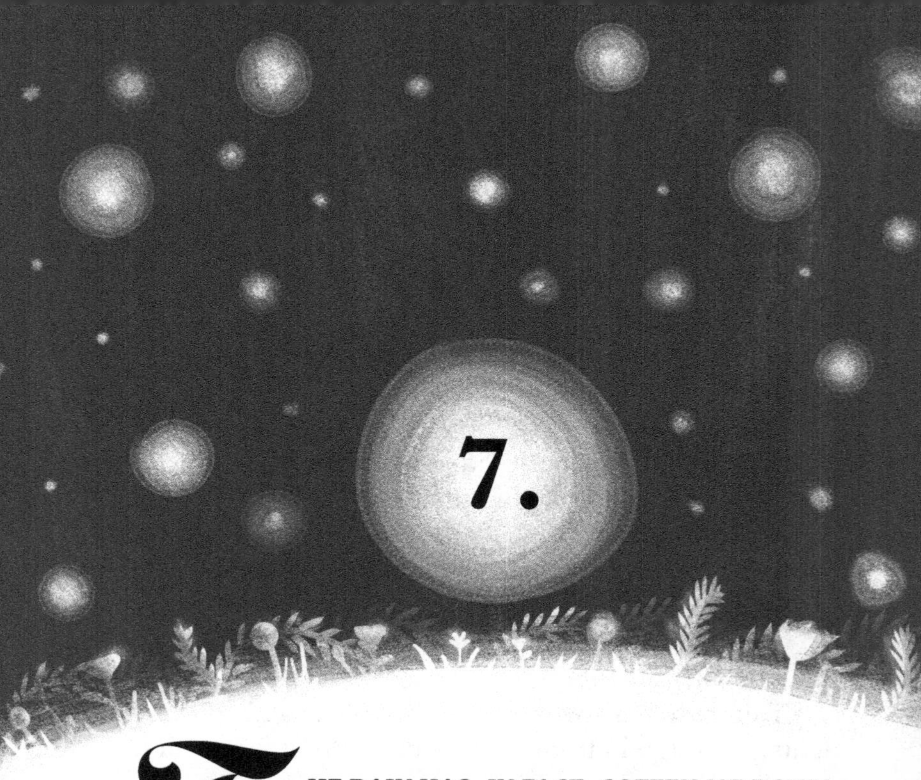

THE RAIN HAS, IN FACT, GOTTEN ME DOWN. When they told me the roof "needed a little work, but nothing serious," they lied through their teeth.

"Again!?" I shout, stepping into yet another puddle.

I've literally designated each of my pots, pans, and bowls for other puddles! I packed too light for all these leaks. It might be dryer if I sleep on the porch.

But I've already woken up there once by accident, and I'm not necessarily eager to do it again.

Gosh, this would absolutely kill as stories on my feed. People love watching mishaps in other people's houses, and at this rate, I'm going to have an indoor pool.

Tree branches scrape against the windows as thunder snaps, making me jump.

7.

God, I'm glad that there aren't any leaks above my record collection. When the power isn't flickering, Fleetwood Mac bounces off the wooden walls, mixing with the sound of the rain.

It would be soothing if I wasn't worried about all the water turning my roof into wet cardboard. If something worse happens, where do I even go? I've always hunkered down with my mom during hurricanes and stuff.

If my power goes out while all the way out here, how long will it take to come back on? I know I wanted to unplug but living without electricity is a little much.

I spring upright at the sound of a crash above my head. It's so terrible I'm convinced the roof is caving. I imagine rain rushing through deep cracks in the ceiling, ugly branches crushing every bit of sentiment I've packed into this place—and me in the process. I need to get out of here.

Rushing out onto the porch, I'm attacked by white sheets of sideways rain. The angry droplets beat down so heavily I can barely see a foot outside the house.

I crane my neck, trying to figure out if something crashed onto the roof. If this cabin isn't safe, I'll have to call Rosie or Chris when the storm blows over; they could take me to the nearest hotel until I can figure out my next move. Hopefully, it won't come to that. I squint at the roofline—I don't think I see any trees.

Water pours down my face, filling my eyes like pools of burning tears. I try to wipe them away, but not before something dark rolls off the side of my house and crashes with a bang.

And as it goes down, my heart catches at the flutter of wings.

Oh my god.

It's my—*the*—forest monster.

My bare feet sink into the mud as I rush toward the body. Blades of wet grass stick to my skin like cat hair to a sweater. His glorious black and yellow wings look somehow wrong. The way they're splayed out upon his back… The left side is somewhat normal, but the right—Oof! The whole wing is folded backward at a sharp angle—there's no doubt it's broken.

His dark feathery antenna flinch with each shallow breath he draws in. His red eyes blink closed and open, closed, and open like a light signaling caution—a warning I ignore when I drag him into my house.

There's no mistaking it.

This is the creature that caught me when I fell from that tree—and yeah, sure, I have no idea *why* he did it, but I'm alive, right? I'll be damned if I leave him outside to die in this storm.

It takes strength I didn't know I had to drag his body inside. Getting him up the stairs is the worst. My nightgown clings to me like a second skin by the time I shuffle to the doorway. Now that he's inside, I have no idea what to do with him. I dry off his exoskeleton with a fluffy towel.

Next, I fold his broken wing against the side of his body. They're softer than they look and delicate, with a pattern similar to a moths. The feathers trickling down from his shoulders are dark, just like the one I found on my walk. My hands shake as I work. One wrong move and I could rip through them like tissue paper. I try to keep the wing in a natural-seeming position, but who knows what that might look like on him.

It takes every bandage in my first aid kit to secure the fragile wing to his body, even then I have to use one of my long silk scarves to finish the job. He wheezes in his sleep, gasping and quaking, his giant body never fully settling.

My experience setting wings starts and ends with the one time my friend Abby and I found a wounded crow in middle school, and honestly, her mom did most of the heavy lifting. This man-bird-bug-creature is a totally different story; my only hope is that he's not too uncomfortable.

The creature's massive body spills across my couch—which is more of a loveseat. I prop up his head with pillows. The tinny sound of water falling into pots and pans reminds me of windchimes as the storm rages outside.

The blanket I drape over his quaking body is too short to cover his legs, so I layer an oversized cardigan to make up the difference. It's endearing in a surreal way. He twitches and groans as he tries to move but eventually settles. What made me so afraid of him that night he held me in his arms? In my memories, he's a demon incarnate, but here, in this cabin, he seems lost.

"You see strange things in the forest," Chris warned me. God, he'd be so pissed at me for not calling him. Despite everything we talked about, I can't bring myself to dial his number.

The creature's red eyes are lipid and dazed like a wounded animal. I watch over him with no regard for my own sopping wet skin or the puddles I'm leaving in my wake. When my teeth start to chatter, I realize letting myself catch a cold is not going to help the situation. I head to my room with caution, stripping off my wet clothes. I slip into plush pajamas, keeping an ear out for the sound of him stirring. Thankfully, by the time I make it back into the living room, his glowing eyes are closed. The rise and fall of his chest assures me that he's still alive. Still, my stomach twists into a knot. I can tell I need to eat, but the idea of food makes me feel even sicker.

Oatmeal is always a safe food—for me at least. It's the one thing my mom always knew to make when I was sick. I wash one of the rain-filled pots and sweeten the oatmeal with honey and cinnamon. I make enough for two, just in case.

When I drizzle in the honey, I notice his fluffy antennae bounce. So, I dish out a second bowl and walk over to where the creature is splayed across my couch.

"You're safe," I whisper.

His eyes droop open in search of my voice, but he gives up, letting them ease shut. Despite the obvious pain he's in, he's allowed himself to relax on to the mountain of pillows I have propped up under his neck.

I raise the glass of water to his… What is that—a beak? Thankfully it doesn't prevent him from drinking. The sound of his stomach grumbling echoes across the cabin.

I guess he's hungry too.

Sliding a spoon past the row of pointed teeth that reside in his beak is only a little unsettling, especially when his eyes crack open, and I can see my reflection in their facets.

7.

I am spoon-feeding a 7-foot moth-creature oatmeal: this is my life now. He eats half the bowl before his half-lidded eyes close again. His breath is heavy and labored; the whole time, his wings flutter as if he's still trying to work through a storm. Whatever is going on inside his head might be something he can't take shelter from.

"I've got you, okay? You're totally fine here," I whisper. I don't know if it's my imagination, but he seems to relax as if I've cast a spell.

He's imposing, yet the way he trembles makes me feel like I've dragged a wounded kitten through my door. A giant, terrifying, bug-like kitten.

I tilt my head, looking at his body. I hope I didn't make the bandages too tight…

His little antennae twitch. They look so soft. I can't resist reaching out and letting my fingertips brush against the soft feather-like bristles.

He jolts up, yanking my hand away. Damn, despite how weak he seemed draped across the couch, his grip is like an iron shackle on my wrist; with every move I make to back away, his long claws dig into my skin.

"Oh my god, will you *chill*?"

His red eyes blink open, but when they land on me, his hand opens. Then, he falls asleep like a toy whose batteries fell out.

I clutch my wrist to my chest and draw in a deep breath. This was probably a bad idea.

8.

I DON'T KNOW WHERE I AM IN THE MORNING. But this time, at least, it's not my porch.

This isn't new. The ceiling here still feels strange, and the smell of damp leaves and rain creeping through the windows is unfamiliar. One day, I'll wake up and this cabin will feel like home, but today is not that day. My body feels like it's been hit by a truck. *Coffee.* Yes, coffee will fix everything. That ridiculous monster hunt must have gotten in my head. Visions from last night's strange dream play through my mind like a movie as I shuffle to the kitchen.

Normally, I take my thyroid medication at least an hour before caffeine but fuck it. My levels have been stable, and I'm beyond exhausted. With each step, I trip over the pots and pans scattered on the floor.

8.

A sharp knock on my door echoes through the cabin. It's too early for visitors. As I walk to the door, my eyes fall on the lump of feathers and claws stirring on my loveseat.

I freeze as the memories of the night before strike like a lightning bolt. It wasn't a dream.

Knock knock knock

My body pivots, unsure of where to turn.

"You okay in there?" I jump at the sound of the low voice—it's muffled but unmistakably Chris. This is just my luck. There's still a 7-foot moth-like creature passed out on my couch—and the local monster hunter is at my door.

I bite down on my bottom lip. Chris seems like a good guy. But this creature is sick—I'm worried he'll treat him like a science experiment or something worse.

I crack open the door just enough so that Chris can see me, but not into the house, I give him my best smile.

"Oh my gosh, hi!" I beam. Mom always said enthusiasm is one of the best ways to mask anxiety, and I guess I'm putting that to the test today. "Did we have plans? I'm totally spacing. It is nice to see you." I inch out of the house until the two of us are toe-to-toe on the porch.

"As dorky as it is, I just wanted to check on you." He looks down at me, his eyes as bright as the sun. "The weather last night got pretty nasty."

Grasping at the opportunity to lead him away from the cabin, I take his arm. The firm muscles under my hand are nothing compared to the monster's—*why am I even comparing the two of them?*

"It's beautiful today, though, isn't it?" I ask, guiding him farther away from my house. "Maybe we could go for a walk or something."

He looks down at me, a half-smile playing across his face. "Okay, what is it?" He shrugs my hand off his arm. Before I can stop him, he's sprinting back up my steps and right to my front door. "Piles of dishes? Boxes overtaking every surface? A mountain of takeout boxes?" He playfully grills me, reaching for the doorknob.

With a theatrical sigh, I fall defeated onto his chest. Is playing into his attraction like this wrong? Probably, but Chris can't find out about the monster in my house—not yet at least.

"All of the above, unfortunately." I hit him with my best puppy-dog eyes, and predictably, his body melts into mine, confirming that

It's working

I'm an absolute tease.

"Please tell me there's a coffee shop somewhere in this town." My head rests in the crook of his shoulder. He's cute, there's no reason I can't flirt with him, and I would really like a decent cup of coffee. Chris's body tenses against mine, and when his blue eyes flicker downward, a heavy blush covers his freckled face.

If he didn't realize I'm wearing a silk nightgown before, he does now.

"Tell you what," he says, not sure where to look. "I'll run out, and you can get back to unpacking."

"My hero." They're just words, but they make him move to his car with strength in his gait, like he's been sent on a noble quest.

"You probably like fancy sugary drinks with plant milk, don't you?" He calls back, crinkling his nose in disgust.

"I very much do!" I refuse to be ashamed of making my coffee taste like ice cream "Iced, please, with oat milk if it's an option."

He rolls his eyes, but the smile never leaves his face. "You sound like my sister!"

"Guess she's got good taste."

"And an espresso machine in the main house." He winks. "I'll see what I can cook up."

"Oh no—you don't have to."

"Relax! Let me take care of this." Chris waves my concerns away with a swipe of his hand. Of course, I don't want him going through all the trouble, especially when I'd prefer him not to come back at all, but who am I to say no to free espresso? After the night I've had, I deserve a little treat.

Once he's gone, I rush back into the house. When he returns, it'll be even harder to find an excuse to send him away. Keeping Chris busy—and preferably outside—is going to be a challenge.

I try to pull the giant creature into the bedroom, but whatever adrenaline that flowed through me last night is long gone and has left sore muscles in its wake. So, back under the pile of blankets, he goes. After he's sufficiently hidden, I take a step back to inspect my handiwork. The monster's hand catches mine before I can move away. He holds me firmly at his side.

"You don't want me to leave?" I whisper, surprised at the warmth of his clawed hand. In response, the creature simply holds me in place with this small, vulnerable gesture. The wings on his back twitch, barely fluttering beneath the weight of the blankets and his bandages. It reminds me of all those viral videos of dogs running in their sleep.

"I'm going to tuck you in, okay? Someone is coming by that I don't want to see you," I explain, draping more blankets and clothing over top of him until my couch looks like a heap of laundry. It'll be a good enough cover if Chris glances through a window, but I'll still need to do my best to keep him away from the cabin.

I wait anxiously until Chris pulls up, slipping outside before he has a chance to knock. He's carrying two travel mugs of coffee, one in each hand. My mouth waters at the sight of an actual iced latte. Maybe him showing up unannounced isn't the worst thing after all? I get a free coffee and a distraction from the crisis happening inside the cabin.

"Let's sit outside, okay?" I don't wait for a response before leading him away from my door.

"Don't worry so much. I can help you unpack while we drink these." I wish he knew how horribly inconvenient his acts of kindness are. To my absolute horror, Chris ignores the empty rocking chair on the patio. Before I can blink, he's let himself inside my house and is standing in the center of the living room. "You know it's okay to ask for help, right?"

"I'm seriously good."

"And all these pots and pans are?"

"I'd like to think they're a part of the decorative experience."

8.

He sets his coffee down on an end table and begins to roll up his sleeves. "I'm sure I've got a tarp out in my truck. I'll patch things up while you sip on that coffee, okay?" He leans forward in a way that makes me think he's resisting the urge to give me a kiss on the forehead. "I'm sure you're worn out from dealing with this mini flood."

"No!" I am *so* not having two people fall off my roof in less than a 24-hour period. Plus, for all I know, my roof is covered in monster feathers. "I mean, you don't want your coffee getting cold right? We're supposed to drink them together." I take my first sip of the latte he made, and damn, it's so delicious it almost makes the headache he's giving me worth it.

"They're rosemary lattes," he says smugly. "Clara—my sister-in-law—and I made the syrup together last week."

"Bet they'd taste great in the fresh air," I say, inching back toward the door.

Behind Chris, the pile of clothes twitches. They're moving as if they have a heartbeat of their own, fueled by the rise and fall of the creature lying beneath them. The entire pile shifts with a deep groan.

"Gah!" I exclaim in the lowest tone I can manage, hitting my chest with my fist. "Sorry, wow, it is like so dusty in here, right?" Out of the corner of my eye, I notice a clawed hand hanging limply off the side of the sofa.

"Let's open up some of these windows," Chris says, turning toward the couch.

"NO! I mean, like, could you actually get the kitchen window? It was uh–umm–"

"Stuck?" he offers.

"Yes! Stuck! Last night! I barely got it closed."

Chris walks with purpose into the kitchen. How the hell am I supposed to get him out of here? While he fiddles with the window above the sink, I dive toward the couch, safely tucking the creature's hand back under the blankets.

"Want me to tackle that laundry pile next?" Chris asks, striding toward the couch.

"You can't!" I shriek, throwing my arms out wide to block him. He raises an eyebrow, glancing behind me.

"Okay, okay, I get it." Chris chuckles, a grin spreading across his face. "It's not like I've never seen a bra before, but—"

"Oh, my god!" I roll my eyes, lightly shoving him toward the door as he bursts into laughter. He's *such* a dude.

"Can we please just move this outside?" I plead one last time. "I need a break from looking at boxes."

"You win." He shrugs, leading me out onto the porch as if he's the one who owns this place. I decline his help again and again while we drain our cups. After a whole hour of trying to avoid talking about the forest monster or why I left Orlando, Chris finally heads back to his truck.

"I have to admit, that was one of the best lattes I've had in a while," I say, returning the to-go cup to his hands. "Thank you."

"I'll have to drop by more often."

Please don't.

"Just shoot me a text next time, 'kay?" I settle on, giving him a sweet smile.

8.

"That'll only work if you give me your number."

Crap. With a cheeky grin, Chris slides his phone into my hand. I add myself to his contacts, unable to miss the gleam in his eye when our hands touch for just a little longer than intended.

"I'll see you around, okay?" He leans forward as if to give me a kiss on the cheek. I bend backward to avoid the affection. There's no questioning that, aesthetically, he's nice to look at; he's just not my type. This is what I get for toying with his emotions.

Who knew hiding a giant monster in your house could be so exhausting?

Chris looks more than a little crestfallen when he leaves, but I'm sure it's nothing he can't recover from.

"Drive safe!" I call as he pulls away from the cabin. As soon as his truck is completely out of view, I rush back inside to check on the monster. Light streams through the windows, creating a beautiful prism of color. A deep, surprisingly human groan rumbles from the loveseat; the sound sends shivers through me. I gulp, pivoting toward him. At least I know hiding him under all that laundry didn't suffocate him.

Stepping lightly over each pot and pan of water, I peer over the blanket mound to check on him; the blanket that was covering him slips away as he turns from the window. He lets out another painful groan.

This can't be—

A lump rises in my throat as I attempt to take in the sight of him.

The monster he's—he's—really really—*hot.*

9.

THE WINGED CREATURE IN MY HOUSE HAS always been hot. I mean *hello*, he's been burning up ever since I dragged him inside, but as far as I know becoming incredibly good-looking isn't a side effect of a fever.

The monster in front of me has transformed into someone who looks *mostly* human.

His face is as pale as the moon, with gold flecks across his forehead; the same iridescent gold freckles his arms and elbows, as if he'd dipped both his arms in paint. The fluffy moth-like antennae are the same, only now they stick out like two feathers from a mass of dark curls.

I jump back as the monster's hand twitches, my heart pounding at the memory of him snatching my wrist. But God, his claws are pretty; they're pointed at the tips, and matte black, the color extending up his fingertips in a ghoulish ombre. Glancing down at my own nails, I suddenly wish I had gotten some acrylics before moving out here. *No, Heather*, I scold myself. *You are not going to be jealous of the forest monster's manicure.*

His wounded wings remain tucked behind his back, appearing just as awkward and uncomfortable as they had last night. His features are angular and strong with soft lips and impossibly dark eyelashes. This demon of a man looks like he was sculpted in clay and painted in acrylic.

Is he really the same person I brought into my house last night? The sudden transformation begs the question: how much of him is still monster? His chest is built and muscular, glittering with the same gold flecks that cover his face—but the lower half of his body is still obscured by my quilt.

Curiosity pulls me forward, though I'm obviously not going to peek. That would be creepy, and he's entitled to his privacy. While his muscular chest rises and falls with a gentle rhythm, I stay close by unable to take my eyes off of him. I don't move until his tongue peeks between his parted lips, wetting them. He's thirsty again. It's easy to tell now that he doesn't have a beak.

I tip the water glass to his lips, and without opening his eyes, he drinks. His brow is covered with sweat I should be too afraid to mop away. The scratches from where he grabbed me last night still burn, but the compulsion to help him is too strong.

He needs me.

I remain at his side all morning, respectfully making sure the heavy quilt stays in place on his lower half.

Time is measured in small sips of water, and dozens of cold compresses for his burning forehead. The monster's eyes never fully open and the closest thing to words from his mouth are groans. The most I can do is try to make him comfortable.

I'd planned to meal prep soup for the week. It's one of those recipes that's supposed to simmer all day. I step into the kitchen and prep all of the ingredients, unceremoniously dumping them into the crock pot after I rinse all of the rainwater out of it. It's not the cute cozy cooking experience I had pictured, but I think the giant winged man on my loveseat is kind of killing the vibe.

After setting the timer on the crockpot, I pick up my book and settle in the armchair. I read the same paragraph over and over until movement from the loveseat catches my attention.

When his eyelashes flutter, light shifts into his eyes. I lean away, setting my book aside. He may be ridiculously pretty, but it doesn't make him any less dangerous.

The breathtaking man surveys the cabin while flexing his hands, splaying his claws wide upon his bandaged chest. He must be able to tell that I helped him, right? I'm not a threat; he's in my house. I need to be commanding, assert myself.

"Hi," I squeak, popping up out of my seat.

Perfect.

I expect him to startle, but instead, the turn of his head is slow and purposeful. I clasp my hands tightly behind my back as his red eyes meet mine. I realize, suddenly, that they are pretty too.

9.

"You, um, you fell off my roof, so I mean, I think you got caught in that storm and uh—are you feeling okay?" I cringe as the clunky sentence leaves my mouth. As far as first impressions go, I don't think either of us are doing so hot.

He tries to ease himself off the couch but lets out a low guttural groan before falling onto his back, squinting like he can't quite make out what's going on around him.

"I'm not going to hurt you." I raise my hands in the air as a sign that I'm not a threat.

"Do you think yourself capable?" he rasps in a deep voice. It's not exactly the most gracious way to greet a rescuer, but the words are enough to send chills running through me. A voice with a face like that should be illegal.

"I'm pretty scrappy," I joke, flexing my non-existent muscles.

I expect to get some sort of reaction. But his expression is impassive. If anything, he looks through me as though I'm nothing more than a decoration in the room.

"You're too small." He tilts his head, the antennae twitching faster than before.

Excuse me?

5'4" seemed average back home. I've always been more of a pear than an hourglass, but I'm shrinking by the second under his gaze.

"How did you manage it?" he whispers, clutching his forehead like he's waking up from a night of binge drinking. He squeezes his eyes shut. "Getting me inside?"

Oh.

It makes sense he'd be confused about *that.* Thick thighs or not, he's easily twice my size, and my arms are about as strong as two noodles.

"I guess I mostly dragged you," I answer, worried it will somehow upset him. "If you hadn't rolled off the roof, you might still be stuck up there."

"Mhm," he groans. His head tilts back, dark hair falling into his eyes, and an elegant, clawed hand covers his face. This man looks like a painting of the devil come to life.

He tries to stretch his wings and winces with pain.

"Oh god, I've never had to set a wing that big before. Is the bandage too tight?"

Even in this form, his irises are the same vibrant shade of red. It's hypnotic, as if I'm in the presence of a vampire. That being said, he's the one looking at *me* as if I have two heads.

"No."

I sigh, relaxing into the seat opposite of him. At least there's that. "Oh, okay good."

"Good?" His dark eyebrow arches, suggesting I said something wrong.

"Are you hungry?" I made more than enough soup for the two of us.

"That's the most pressing question you have for me?"

"Oh, uh, are you like, comfortable or…?" I literally have no idea what he's trying to say.

"You do not—" The little furry antenna on his head bounce impatiently as if he's expecting me to ask a question off a test I didn't study for.

"*What?*"

He huffs, crossing his arms.

No response. *Awesome.*

If I wanted this kind of judgment, I would have stayed on social media. Feeling more than a little frustrated with his attitude, I dish him up a bowl of lackluster soup, placing it next to him on the end table. A pained hiss seethes from between his fangs as he reaches for the bowl.

"Here." I raise a shaking spoon to his lips. We repeat the ritual, bite after bite, and eventually, my nerves begin to settle. The creature continues to stare at me as if I'm the weird one in this situation but doesn't refuse my help. "What's your name?"

It's not much of a surprise when he doesn't answer.

"Well, I'm Heather—in case you're wondering who, y'know, saved your life or whatever." The name feels just as odd as it did when I introduced myself to Rosie and Chris. His expression doesn't change. I wonder if he even heard me.

The silence is finally broken by a labored breath. "Heather?" The name rolls off his tongue as smooth as silk. He pauses as if he's mulling something over but does not speak again for a long moment. "*Saved my life,* did you?"

I tilt my head. There's a bite to the words, as if he's angry to be here, safe and warm in my house.

"Uh... duh? Anyways! You can just like chill now, okay?" I pace the length of the couch where he's sprawled out; it's impossible not to stare at him. His long lashes flutter closed. He looks almost angelic. "Relax, get your strength up or whatever. I like just can't even imagine—and I have so many questions, but for now just—oh! Should we move you to the bed? It's just a queen, but you'd have more room while you're here and um, well—"

He's staring at me again, unblinking.

Oh cool, I'm rambling in front of the ethereal forest hottie.

The thing is, I can't stop talking; his lack of response is only making it worse. Only when his head lolls to the side, and the only sound in the room is his heavy breathing, do my words run dry.

I fight the urge to sweep his dark curls away from his brow. Now that we've properly met, I don't think the gesture would be welcome. Despite the whole saving his life thing, he doesn't seem to want anything to do with me.

"Foolish," he rasps under his breath. I choose to believe he's talking in his sleep, not insulting me—*again.*

So much for gratitude.

10.

THE WINGED MAN IS IN AND OUT OF CONSCIOUSNESS for the next two days; he mostly sleeps and begrudgingly lets me check on him. It's awkward, to say the very least.

I still have no idea who he is, *what* he is, or if anything I've done so far is actually helping. To make matters worse, he doesn't seem to like to be fussed over. Which is too damn bad because he's in my house, and I'm not going to have him get sicker under my watch.

"Are you feeling any better?" I ask, raising a spoonful of soup to his lips.

He practically grunts in response.

"Your fever seems like it's broken."

His dark eyes flicker to meet mine for just a moment before turning his attention back to the window.

I wonder if he can hear my heart pounding.

Another few sips of water.

A few bites of soup.

It's a relief when he's able to raise a shaky hand to his own lips. He's too stubborn to ask for my help, but he also doesn't refuse when I offer. Though, that in no way means we're getting along. If I had a dollar for every time he spoke to me, it wouldn't even cover my Starbucks order.

He's stubborn, quiet, grumpy, with eyes that set my entire soul on fire. I can barely look in his direction without feeling myself blush. I don't know how to feel about it— especially since I'm pretty sure he hates me.

Spending a few hours outside sounds like a break, even if my grand plan involves patching up the roof. I'm beyond lucky to find an old tarp and somewhat sturdy ladder in the shed. With another forecast of rain for this evening, today is the day to get the job done. I seriously don't want to clean up another round of rain-filled pots and pans.

"You will not climb up there," the creature gruffly orders from across the room.

"I won't?" I pause, slowly pivoting toward my unwanted houseguest.

He braces himself on the arm of the couch as he rises to his feet. The quilt slips away, and for the first time, I get a look at the lower half of his body as he stalks towards me. The exoskeleton clings like armor to his legs, it climbs up his waist like a mermaid's scales. If I squint, it's like he's wearing a pair of dark leggings— but he's not.

The monster standing toe-to-toe with me is naked—*I think*. Heat rises to my face; if he's not going to make it weird, neither am I, even if my whole body feels like it's flushed pink. I crane my neck to look up at his devilishly handsome face, suddenly aware of how much taller than me he is. His back curves so that he doesn't hit his head on the cabin's low ceiling.

"It is dangerous."

He couldn't possibly be worried about me, could he? He's been so aloof this whole time. I don't want to give him the satisfaction of seeing me flattered. But when I look into his glowing red eyes, I freeze. God, he's looking at me like someone who's worried their favorite coffee cup is going to fall off of a tall shelf. His wide eyes scan over me, inspecting every imperfection, every crack that might cause me to break under pressure.

I shake it off.

After days of indifference, I'm not sure he's allowed to look at me like that.

"Oh please, this one time I basically hung off the balcony of this three-story balcony for an influencer campaign, high heels in one hand, a mimosa in the other. It was just a prop, but I was holding on with what? An elbow? I can handle a one-story roof. Besides—" With dramatic flair, I spin and kick out my right foot. "—I'm wearing work boots." Maybe it's the pink glitter covering my shoes or that I tripped over my skirt during my spin, but he looks less than convinced.

We're locked in a stand-off until his large body begins to sway like a large oak tree.

"Whoa, careful!" Following my reckless instincts, I catch his waist to steady him. The man stares down at

me with an unreadable expression that doesn't budge when I bring him back to the couch.

"What is it you've done to me?" His voice is a velvet whisper that makes my blood run cold.

"I told you—if, uh, the bandages are too tight, I can—"

With a thud, he collapses onto the cushions and the air of mystery is broken with a glare. Obviously, he's upset about more than just the bandages. "I *should* be healed by now."

Okay, sure, it must be frustrating, but I'm doing my best here! In his frustration, he makes a feeble attempt to rise again. He stands too quickly and bumps his head on the rafters.

He's currently the one thing standing in the way of my simple life out here in the woods. Despite being a pain to take care of, I'd rather he wait until he's fully healed before charging out into the woods.

I watch his dark black claws splay in a cat-like stretch. I don't get it. This man could snap anyone in half—he could snap me in half—but it's more than that making my heart race. How could someone like him be taken out by a storm?

Absentmindedly, I trail my fingers along the claw marks on my wrist, and the man—or monster, I'm not sure what to call him anymore—catches my arm in his hand and studies the marks with a grimace.

"You are hurt."

If I didn't know better, I'd think he's poised to go after my attacker—which would be awkward considering it was, you know, him. His red eyes turn from ruby to deep crimson as he considers the scratch marks.

10.

"Who did this?" The guttural tone he emits is low and dangerous. I wonder if he can feel the goosebumps forming on my skin under his fingertips.

"Uh, you. Sorry, I think I startled you the first night." I force a laugh, and oh my god my heart is going to explode. "It's no big."

He visibly softens, his grip loosening as if suddenly unsure whether his touch is welcome. Slowly, his index finger trails along the marks. "It is a big."

A strange laugh escapes me. The phrasing he chose sounds surprisingly cute.

"You didn't draw blood or anything." I yank my arm away, clasping my hands behind my back. "Besides, since when are you like *so* worried about me?"

"If you will permit me to take a look," he urges, ignoring my commentary completely. He waits until I offer him my arm again before seizing my wrist; he presses a kiss to my wound.

I don't understand.

Why would he—?

"Heather?" My chest flutters at the sound of my name from the lips that just kissed me. When he draws back, I catch a glimpse of his pointed teeth and freeze. No—nope this is not happening.

I avert my attention, pretending to look for something on the counter. Keys? No, I don't need my keys. A flashlight? It's broad daylight. What do people take up on roofs with them? I aimlessly pace through the tiny kitchen, avoiding making eye contact.

"That was your name..." His voice trails off like he doesn't trust himself to remember. His day has probably felt like a weird blur, consisting only of sleep and being spoon-fed by a stranger.

"Mmhmm," I mumble, drawn back in by his ruby eyes. The problem isn't that he kissed me. It's that I want him to do it again.

"Are you a witch?"

It takes an hour before I stop laughing at the ridiculous question. Sure, I dabble in a "witchy" aesthetic every fall, and I've certainly been called worse online. But an *actual* witch? No. The only magic I have is being able to write a damn good caption and apparently putting a tarp on a roof with minimal damage to my shoes. I mean, did I almost fall off the roof three times? Yes. Is the tarp secured tightly to prevent further leaking? Yes, I think so. Honestly, I have no idea, but it's as good as it's going to get.

Magic might be an overstatement.

When I breeze back into the house, I expect my guest to criticize me. But instead, his large body hangs off the loveseat, with his chin tucked to his chest. It reminds me of how you'd fall asleep on an airplane. If I had a little neck pillow, it might help. He stirs, blinking sleepily in my direction, before straightening up.

"Will you be good for like, an hour-ish?" As if casting a spell on him, I wiggle my fingers. "I need to restock my potions." The idea of leaving him here by himself is daunting, but if I have to eat another bowl of soup, I'm going to scream. We need groceries.

"You speak as if I have a choice." He makes a melodramatic motion toward his broken wing. Ugh, this forest monster is seriously *such* a baby.

"Again, I think the words you're looking for are 'thank you.'" How can he seriously be so rude? "You act like I should have just left you out in the rain..."

"And because I saved you that night, you did not?" A strange tension hangs in the air between us. His eyes search through me as if looking for more than just an answer.

"You were hurt." What does he think I should have done: just leave him out there?

"That's all it took?" He looks at me from under his impossibly long lashes.

"Well, yeah." I shrug. "What else would I need?"

The winged man doesn't answer. I'm glad to know my company is less preferable than dying in the freezing rain. I turn my body away from his, finally breaking eye contact.

"Most would have pretended I did not exist." His low voice comes as a surprise, sending a warm shiver up my spine. My thoughts drift to Chris and his overzealous monster hunting group. I laugh.

"I seriously doubt that."

11.

JUST HOPPING IN MY CAR AND DRIVING away from the house feels weird, knowing the monster from the woods is just sitting on my couch … existing.

His fever has broken, and I don't think anything will happen exactly; it's just *odd*. I'd typically just order delivery if company was over, but I'm not sure that the giant winged man counts as a guest.

I need to figure out what to call him.

He looks like he'd be named something mysterious like Damian or Raven or, oh, maybe Klaus. But, no, *no*, he's not a puppy; I can't randomly pick something that I think sounds cute. I can't buy him little—*big*—knitted sweaters and take silly photos for Christmas cards. Jesus, I need to make more friends.

11.

The General Store is the closest place for groceries, and as weird as it feels to potentially run into Chris considering I'm harboring what he'd consider a monster, I don't really want to drive an hour to Walmart.

I'm relieved when I don't see his dark red truck in the parking lot. When I peer inside, it's just Rosie perched behind the counter reading a book. The store is perfectly empty.

"Oh, hey!" She greets me with a charming toothy grin. "How's the move treating you?"

"Yeah, good," I chuckle. "Totally normal so far." I shift away from her bright-eyed gaze to examine a display of homemade preserves sitting on one of the shelves.

"Sorry again about my brother," she says with a shake of her head. "I know he can be a bit much."

"Oh, it's seriously no big." I brush off her apology, navigating the aisles. I pick up a bag of apples, a carton of orange juice, and a couple of tomatoes. I have olives at home and could totally make cashew cheese in the food processor. I brought my food processor, right? I think I remember unpacking it. God, I hate moving.

"If there's ever anything you need produce-wise, feel free to call ahead," Rosie says, leaning over the counter. "If it's in season, I'll bring something in special for you."

"Oh, that's right; you said you and your wife have a farm nearby, right?"

"Yeah, she oversees it while I'm here. She likes plants and animals more than people." Rosie smirks, shrugging her shoulders. Most of the good couples I know have a designated extrovert. I guess that must be her.

"Relatable."

The two of us laugh, even though it's not particularly funny. When I make it to the counter, she tries to upsell me banana bread, which I have to unfortunately turn down.

"I would if I could, believe me." My mouth waters just looking the fluffy loaf of chocolate chip goodness. There was a bakery back home in Orlando that made the best gluten-free treats. Ugh, I should have stocked up before moving. I wonder if my house guest likes banana bread...

"So, about the whole lunch thing." Rosie's soft voice snaps me back to reality. "I realized that I never got your number." Oh wow. She still actually wants to hang out, even after my awkward not-a-date with her brother. I haven't been to a farm since I was a kid. Seeing baby animals and getting to help in the garden is tempting. Sure, I came out here to be alone, but with a giant forest creature living in my house, that's kind of a bust anyway. I might as well take her up on her offer.

"Yeah, text me, and we'll figure it out." The two of us exchange numbers, and I head back home with groceries and a possible new friend. I see no sign of Chris.

Win, win, and another win.

My mysterious creature is sound asleep again when I arrive home. He stirs only slightly at the sound of dinner being cooked—even the *brrr* of the food processor. The cute antennae on his head bobble at the sound, but my houseguest's eyes stay firmly closed.

It's nothing fancy, just the gluten free noodles I thankfully packed along with my meager rations from home, homemade cashew cheese, and olives. I place an overflowing bowl of pasta on the end table next to him and retreat to my bedroom with a giant bowl of noodles in hand. It's not like I was counting on good conversation, but sitting in my room alone, I sink into thoughts that would have been better left in my old apartment in Florida.

Everyone is probably living it up at home. From what my mom has told me, there's no shortage of rumors about my disappearance. Gossip spread like wildfire in my old social circles. I've given them the gift of something to whisper about at all the parties.

My stomach flips at the thought of how many cute bakery openings I'm missing. What has everyone been up to since I swore off social media forever? Is my mom trying out new recipes? Gosh, if I was home, she probably would have called me to be a taste tester.

The pasta I've been shoveling in my mouth suddenly seems bland compared to the leftovers Mom would send home with me. When she was in her cake decorating phase, my freezer overflowed with her delicious "failures" for at least six months. But more than the food, I miss *her.*

It wouldn't take much to check in on her.

I wouldn't even have to call.

I just have to log in for a minute—just a minute—and then log right off. No, I can't. I've been so good. And honestly, I'm not sure that I miss any of it, really … but what if someone *misses me*? I could have a DM from one of my old friends begging me to come home. But no—I won't break. I just need a distraction, and there's a perfect one sitting with broken wings on my couch.

Rain gently taps on the old windows; the winged man watches it with as much fascination as someone taking in their favorite television show.

"I can't believe it's raining again." I stretch my arms up to the sky, stealing a glance in his direction. A lump forms in my throat. He really has no business being so handsome. "I'm glad the tarp on the roof seems like it made a difference."

"I cannot believe you did not fall." The richness of his voice is a treat that catches me off guard every time. But damn, his holier than thou attitude is getting a little old.

"I would hate to steal your signature move." I wink, claiming my seat in the floral armchair opposite him. It's become my spot ever since he took over the loveseat.

"You forget our first meeting." He whispers, and is that a *smirk* on his lips? I shake it off. Still, something about him is fascinating. He doesn't speak or act like someone who has spent their entire life in the wilderness. No, there's something regal about his tone, an air of arrogance like someone who's never heard the word *no*. This man sounds as if he's lived a million lifetimes, and in all of them, he's been a prince.

"Guess we both keep falling for each other." The words slip from my lips before I can stop them. In response, he openly gapes at me, which is like fair, I guess.

Note to self: *do not flirt with the forest monster again.* I study the pattern of his wings. The feathers only line the rim; the rest is delicate and paper-thin, a dark shade of black with symmetrical yellow spots on each corner. All this time the pattern has reminded me of the wings of a moth.

"If you're not going to tell me your name, can I call you Moth?" It's not the most original, but from someone who named their first cat *Potato*, it could be worse. May she rest in peace.

"It does not matter what I am called."

"But you wouldn't *dislike* it?" I press.

"I would not."

Well, that's something.

To defuse the tension, I offer him a cookie from the open tin. He ignores it, but I think I see a twitch in his fingers as if he's second-guessing himself. I follow his gaze out the window, watching the droplets of water puddle on the lawn. We haven't talked about why he was near my house the night of the storm—or the night I thought he was trying to kill me.

"Why did you come back here?" I'd assumed it was a coincidence, but now, seeing the way he's averting his eyes, I'm not so sure. "Like, why were you even near the cabin at all? You caught me when I fell and brought me back here— "A grin spreads across my face as I make a stunning realization. "Oh my gosh, you came to check on me, didn't you?" I squeak, leaning forward in my chair so that my face is dangerously close to his.

"I take care of the helpless creatures in these woods." Moth rolls his eyes as if I'm no one important. *God.* It's like living with one of my internet trolls. I should have stayed in my room staring at the ceiling—anything would be better than trying to have a conversation with him.

"Fine! Tomorrow, you can feed *me* soup." I throw the tin of cookies on the counter. He can have them all for all I care. I've suddenly lost my appetite.

I storm to my bedroom, feeling like a sullen teenager, but instead of blasting music and angrily writing in a journal, I take refuge under the covers.

Maybe he'll just leave. He doesn't seem completely better, but he has improved. When I wake up, this whole thing could feel like a weirdly thankless dream.

The light from my phone illuminates the dark bedroom, casting a shadow on the dusty corners I missed when I was cleaning. Until this moment, I hadn't realized how empty this room feels despite the flowers, garlands, and clutter. The light draws me closer, tempting me with its glow.

Maybe I'll just look for a second.

I shouldn't log in. I know that. But my fingers tap the all-too-familiar password, and now, I'm staring at a wall of notifications.

@HoneyBeaFAN1: *"Where's recipe Wednesday??"*
@ Anon456: *"I think she's embarrassed to show her face (literally) after the Babely scandal"*

I would hardly call that a scandal, but I guess it was the straw that finally broke me.

@TayTay768: *"Miss you, queen!!"*
@OliverSnoops55: *"You owe us an explanation. Without your followers and your mommy's help, you would be nowhere."*

11.

@PumpkinPaige: *"Unfollowed a while ago, her content is just so fake."*
@Anon890: *"She's probably taking a break."*
@Anon321: *"From what? Wearing pretty clothes and lounging by the pool? LOL! If only my life was that easy. I'm working three jobs and can barely make rent."*
@ Anon789: *"Watch her come back after a week talking about her #unplugged luxury Airbnb weekend"*
@LouieLou234*: "Lolol just needed to relax without technology! Watch the whole vacation on my Patreon."*
@SunshineNFlower421: *"She has the cutest baby bump! I hope her and Jace go public soon."*
@HoneyLatteFanz1: *"Honey and Jace OTP"*
@HoneyBeaFans5: *"I bet she's working on a cool secret project! HoneyBea, come back online!! We all miss you!"*
@Anon890: *"Does sis have a patron?"*
@LouieLou234: *"I was making a joke"*
@Anon321: *"Ew, her skin looks nasty."*
@InsultBot54: *"You know you don't have to post everything, right?"*
@JaceNHoneyFans: *"Chase that dollar, girl"*
@TeaNCupcake3: *"Lol I see there's no #freshfacefriday this week."*
@HoneyLatteFanz: *"Lay off, everyone! She's probably working."*
@Anon321: *"Lol doing what?"*

It's somehow worse than I was expecting. With a groan, I toss my phone across the bed and burrow under my blankets. I pointedly ignore my overflowing DMs and emails—for the moment, at least.

But I can't help myself. I pick up my phone again and scroll and scroll; my heart feels like it's getting torn out of my chest. The cruelty in my comment section overshadows any kindness.

Gossip blogs are talking about how I ghosted the entire internet.

My mom has put out a statement asking people to respect my privacy; she's not comfortable speaking for me or answering my follower's questions.

"My HoneyBea is taking a little digital detox, but she'll be back soon," she writes at the end of a long heartfelt post before sharing a pre-order link to her next cookbook. Bless her for never missing an opportunity to hustle. Mom still doesn't realize that I don't think I want to come back.

I shouldn't even be scrolling right now.

No one wants me online—or here, for that matter.

After scrolling until my eyes are bloodshot, I feel like I was hit by a truck. My joints ache from lack of sleep. Sunlight streams through the window, causing me to burrow deeper into my blanket fortress. When did my dream life become such a nightmare?

There are leftovers in the fridge and snacks on the counter. My houseguest can take care of himself today. Instead of making breakfast like usual, I sink into the mattress, tightly cocooning myself in the soft blankets.

Work? What does she even do?

Nothing. Absolutely nothing of value, at least. And that's what I'm going to continue to do all day.

Heaviness builds in my chest until boulders are resting on top of me. They keep me pinned tight to the mattress, awake and frozen in place. I don't sleep, and when I do, it's over before it's begun.

There's a blog post I wrote about dealing with situations like this: "10 Ways to Turn Around Any Bad Mood!" It's one of my most popular pieces.

I should go outside.

I should listen to music.

I should put on an old movie.

I should unpack and bake something. Baked goods always make me feel better.

I should do something—anything.

Instead, I roll over and burrow tighter in the blankets, proving each of the commenters right. I'll sink into the mattress until I dissolve into a pile of cheap glitter and ash.

I squeeze my eyes tight. My stomach twinges. The clock blinks 2:30 p.m. I haven't eaten anything yet, but I don't know that I'm hungry. If I was, I'd pull myself out of bed, right?

I'm not hungry, but I nibble. I check on my begrudging houseguest from time to time and close myself in my room with handfuls of granola bars.

I feel like garbage—because I am. Absolute and utter garbage. Who, mind you, has made it very clear she does not want to be disturbed. Yet, there's a creaking at my door.

Moth looms just outside of my door. He hunches his shoulders, so his head doesn't hit the ceiling. I

wonder if the way he's standing is making his wing hurt even more. I decide that I don't care.

"You are unwell." He blinks slowly, the antennae on his head bobbling as he moves toward me. It would be cute if I was paying attention to those things; I also *definitely* don't notice how his gold-flecked skin looks like stars painted across a fresh snowfall.

"I'm fine."

"Mmmffph," he hums, unconvinced. A clawed hand reaches out, and before I can move, presses down gently upon my forehead.

"I—" I can't think. If I didn't feel warm before, I do now. Heat radiates off my face with every second his palm stays pressed against my skin. I've done this to him dozens of times, but it's different somehow. I haven't done anything to deserve this sort of attention.

"Like I said, I'm seriously fine." I roll away, unable to stand the warm sensation building inside me. "There's food in the fridge."

"Understood."

The floorboards creak beneath his feet as he shuffles away from my bed and back into the living room. I sigh, burrowing back under the blankets. There was something unexpectedly tender about how his fingertips had brushed against my skin, very unlike the man who has only grunted two words in my direction. He should be using this as his excuse to "escape the witch of the woods" since that's what he thinks I am.

Now that I'm alone, the siren's call of my phone taunts me from the edge of the bed.

Maybe I should get a landline, then my temptation would be gone.

Service sucks out here anyway.

No more emails, text messages, alerts, or feeds to scroll through. That would fix everything, wouldn't it? I didn't move all the way out here to doom scroll from under the covers.

The thud of something heavy being set on the nightstand makes me shrug off my blankets. Moth is back for some reason—just who I wanted to witness my depression spiral.

"Can you not just loom over my bed?" I snap, refusing to look at him.

"What would you prefer I do?"

"Whatever you want."

"And if I want to loom?"

"Just sit down or leave!" I shriek.

His answer comes in the form of unexpected weight on the left side of my bed. There he is, perched on my floral sheets with an apple in-hand. I stare up at him. Before I can open my mouth to speak, he slices a wedge clean off the core with his claw and presses it to my lips.

"What are you—?"

"You have not eaten."

I take a bite; sweet and crisp juices slide across my tongue. He cuts another piece with his claws and offers it to me. Tears well up in my eyes. I can't deal with this right now.

"You are hurt?" he asks, his deep voice surprisingly gentle.

"Yeah," I answer honestly, glancing back at my discarded phone.

"Will you eat?"

I nod slowly, taking the rest of the apple from his hands.

I wait for him to leave. Instead, he settles in next to me; he doesn't say much but I have to admit, it's nice not to be alone. Along with the apple, he'd set a bowl of soup on the nightstand. I stare down at the same blend of vegetables we've been eating every day. My stomach twists.

"Moth…"

"That is the name you have bestowed on me."

"I think I hate soup."

"It is not very good," he admits, his wings flopping in a cartoonish manner with the casual shrug of his shoulders.

"All the cute, cozy cabin influencers always made it look so relaxing and–and I'm sorry, *what* did you just say?"

"I merely agreed; why are you angry?"

"I said I hate soup! Not that it wasn't good." I take a small spoonful and grimace at the blend of mushy vegetables on my tongue. Okay, no. I hate this so much.

"It is not entirely intolerable."

"You don't need to try to cheer me up." I groan. "But hey, I'm glad we found something in this house you dislike at least a little more than me."

"You … are not entirely intolerable." The words spill from him so quietly I'm not sure that I heard him correctly.

"It just feels like it's a part of the cute-girl-in-the-woods package, y'know?" I sigh. "I love a flowy dress, and besides the horrible roof, the cabin is great. But I'm supposed to be in a linen apron stirring—and ah, it's not like you care at all. God, I can't even unplug correctly."

"Who for?"

"What?"

"Who is your terrible soup for?" He pinches the bridge of his nose as if the mere act of speaking to me is a chore. "We are the only two here. I do not think you toiling away to create food you dislike makes you… What was it you called yourself?"

He avoids calling me a cute-girl-in-the-woods, and I'm not going to repeat myself. I'm cute. I live in the woods. He can deal with it. Still, he does have a point. I'm not online performing life anymore. So why do I feel like I'm supposed to fit into some neat outdoorsy mold? I drag my knees up to my chest. "A lot of people really don't like me," I tell him. "I thought you might be one of them."

"I am not people." He eyes the apple with a raised eyebrow. "Now, eat."

Moth doesn't take his eyes off me, watching like a hawk studying its prey. It makes me nervous. Hasn't he ever seen someone eat an apple before? He seems satisfied only when it's been nibbled down to the core. He turns to leave, and I reach out, my fingers tracing along his wrist before it moves just out of reach.

He gazes down at me with those gemstone eyes, and I gulp

Why do you suddenly care so much? I want to ask, but the question snags on my lips. I can't bear to hear that he doesn't.

This is the most looked after I've felt in—*God*—months? And I need it, insults and all. I want to make it stretch out as long as possible.

"Could you stay?" I brace myself for the sting of rejection—a cold laugh or a smug remark. Instead, he somehow squeezes into a space next to me. His warmth is all-encompassing and comfortable; he's very easy to relax into, like a giant heated body pillow.

"It's not a big deal—you don't have to, but I'm tired of being alone," I say, pulling away just enough to tuck a blanket between us. Something in that statement must connect because his body stays firmly next to mine.

"I will stay." The words are softer than a million goose down pillows and even sweeter coming from his lips. I don't understand why he's being so tender. Instead of questioning it, I melt into the feeling of his body against mine.

Finally, after what feels like days, I fall asleep.

12.

WHEN I ASKED MOTH TO STAY, I MEANT like, for a little while, not *all night.* His heart thumps like the beat of a drum under my ear, which is pressed firmly against his chest. All things considered, I'm surprised at how comfortably we fit together. Under my body, he's so soft and alive—despite his whole dark forest prince appearance, he really is just a man, isn't he? When he isn't a monster, that is...

My fingers trail up the length of his chest. His dark lashes fly open with a sharp intake of his breath.

"Ah!" I squeak, leaping off of him. "I'm so sorry. I didn't realize. I shouldn't have."

"I did not mind." His voice lacks warmth, but I swear that I spot a smirk on his lips for just a moment.

"Breakfast! Toast! Toast is good, right?" I don't wait for his reply before I charge toward the kitchen.

"Have I misunderstood?" he calls.

"I'm sorry?" I pause at the threshold, clutching the doorjamb.

"You asked me to lie with you last night."

"Oh my god! Don't say it like that." My face is burning. He knows I just wanted–well, I don't know what I wanted. But I didn't ask him to do *that*.

I know for a fact that nothing happened.

"Did you not wish for me to share your bed?"

"You are doing that on purpose!"

I expect a sly smirk or crooked smile to play on his lips, but this man is entirely sincere. He doesn't even blink. The feeling of his body pressed against mine echoes across my skin. Since the whole "clothes" thing has been ambiguous, I have made it a point to not stare at the lower half of his body. Keeping my eyes off of his bare chest has been hard enough as it is. But most of the time, he's languishing on my couch covered in blankets. Only now do I see the curve of his very grabbable-looking butt peeking out from under the cover of his bandaged wings. I can't stand to look at the utter perfection of his body for one more second. I rush into the kitchen, cheeks burning, and slot four slices of bread into the toaster.

"You are feeling better?" he asks. With long strides of his impossibly muscular legs, Moth has followed me, and I suddenly wish this cozy cabin was double the size.

"Huh? What? Yeah, no, I'm fine." When the toast pops, I divide them onto two plates, claiming a piece and taking a hasty bite. It's dry and crumbly in my mouth; In my haphazard rush, I didn't add jam or butter, and the texture only adds to the lump forming in my throat.

There's no way he's that clueless…

"Why would you be worried about some forest witch anyway?"

"You are *my* forest witch." His statement is not followed by laughter.

This ethereal man just called me *his*. And I'm sure I must have misheard him. I just about swallow the rest of my dry bread whole before taking my plate to the sink. How am I supposed to collect myself when he keeps saying things like that?

When I turn back, he's carefully easing himself into one of my small dining chairs. It looks as though someone crammed a G. I Joe in a Barbie dream house. His legs don't quite fit under the table and splay open in a way that again has me taking in just how muscular he is. I slide his plate across the table, not wanting to stand too close to him.

Moth's hands make my already minuscule gluten-free slices of bread look like appetizers. And when his gaze dips down for a moment, I'm reminded of how impossibly long his eyelashes are.

"You can eat what's at the table!" I practically sprint to the bathroom to splash cold water on my face. Thankfully, I have a text from Rosie to distract myself with. Lunch out at her farm will be the perfect excuse to get away from Moth while I sort out these feelings.

I need to pull myself together—but more than that, I need to get him to tell me more about himself. What is it that he does all the way out here? Lurking around the forest like a handsome ghost, whispering on the wind? I mean, live your best life, right? But there's got to be more to it than that. I return to the kitchen, turning my phone in my hands.

"So…" I have no idea how to phrase the question I want to ask. I rock back and forth on my heels, trying to think of the words. I find Moth perched on the table, his fangs plunged into the hem of my lace tablecloth.

"What the actual fuck," I breathe.

He opens his jaw, and the fabric slides back into place, kissed at the edges by his teeth. "I—"

"Are you literally *eating* my tablecloth?"

"It was—"

"What … an accident? How do you accidentally eat a tablecloth?" I can't deal with this right now. My phone pings with a message that I ignore, keeping my eyes fixed on Moth's flushed face.

"You said I was permitted to eat what was on the table."

"The *food*! Oh my god."

"It is your fault for not being specific." His fangs flash in what I think might be a smirk. Is he … messing with me right now?

"Oh my god." I don't know if I want to laugh or cry at the stupidity of the situation. *This!* This is his attempt at humor? "Literally! I'm just staring at you like, 'wow, how does this god of a man exist,' and then you eat my tablecloth?!" I shout, shaking my head. Then I freeze, realizing what I just said. You know what? No. I am not going to be the one who is embarrassed here. Maybe I was wrong to ask him to stay with me last night, but the man is still clearly high on cough syrup. I'm just glad he's starting to feel better.

"I believed it would make you laugh."

"Aw, humor is apparently just not your thing, babe." I stick my tongue out, realizing I just called Moth both a god of a man, cute, and babe in less than a minute. My lunch with Clara and Rosie cannot come soon enough. I need out of this house.

Another ping from my phone pulls my attention away.

[Rosie: Should I invite Chris today?]

I blush, reading his name. *Crap.* There's no way I want to see him today. He's her brother, though; I need to make sure I'm not being a dick about it.

[Me: Yeah, I mean, he's super sweet, but we just didn't really vibe.]

[Rosie: I keep telling him a "Monster Hunt" isn't a suitable first date.]

I hide my phone from Moth as I type. It's not like he and I are … anything. I don't even think he likes being around me.

He'll be gone as soon as his wings are healed, and I'll be in this tiny cottage by myself again.

That being said, I don't want him to know that just days ago I was stomping through the woods, hunting him with his #1 fanboy.

[Me: I mean, everyone has their hobbies, I guess.]

I crinkle my nose, letting my hair fall forward.

[Me: Just not really into the whole mysterious creature from the forest thing.]

I catch Moth's ruby eyes and sigh.
"Yes?" he asks, his long lashes fluttering.
"I can't zone out in my own house?"
"You are staring."
"Kinda the whole thing with zoning out."
"Hmm." His soft-looking lips purse.
"Hmm!" I echo, turning my shoulders sharply away; I can see his reflection in the mirror. A small smile curves his lips.
Maybe I should stare more often.

THERE'S SOMETHING ABOUT ROSIE AND Clara's farm that feels familiar and comfortable. Their old farmhouse is shabby-chic and charming. Within minutes I'm utterly relaxed as I sink into a sage-green velvet armchair, gingerly snagging a cookie from the tray in front of me.

"We made them with almond flour!" Rosie announces, taking the seat opposite of me.

"You two are literal angels!"

They are beautiful, kind, welcoming, and completely head over heels for each other in a way that makes whatever school-girl-crush I had on Rosie sink into the back of my brain.

I want someone to look at me like that.

"So, where did you move from?" Clara asks, her brown eyes sparkling underneath her teal glasses. The vibrant color pops against her tan skin. Her hair is a similar shade of teal with dark roots. She sets the tray of beautiful-looking cookies in front of me on the coffee table, and my stomach rumbles in response.

"Orlando. I traded theme parks and coffee shops for the great outdoors." I force a small smile.

"Shut up! I'm from there!" Clara squeals. "Rosie and I met while she was in the Disney College program. We did the parks for our honeymoon."

"Yup, matching ears and everything," Rosie adds.

"Aw, I love that for you two." I bite into the cookie, and cinnamon and sugar explodes across my tongue. "These are perfect."

We laugh about everything from Horror Nights and parades to the weird wizard tourist trap while Rosie laments about how much she misses the sunshine.

I can't relate. The humidity made it feel like I stepped into a dishwasher every time I ventured outside. However, my heart pines for coffee shops, bakeries, and craft markets. There was something so perfect about getting a fancy latte with friends before walking down my favorite strip to hunt for vintage treasures—then ending the day with ice cream or donuts.

The more we talk, the more I realize I might miss food more than I miss people. Considering Jace and the rest of my so-called "friends," maybe that's entirely fair.

"Oh my god, if you sold these at the store, I'd be buying like two boxes a week," I say after inhaling yet another cookie. The classic flavor pairs so well with the rosemary latte I'm sipping. This farmhouse might be my new favorite place for coffee—if this becomes a regular thing, that is.

"I'm so glad. If I'm being honest, I stressed a little while I was making them." Clara's tattoo-covered shoulders relax as Rosie drapes an arm around her waist. Her grin is toothy, and when Clara glances over, I notice that she blushes. These two are so cute, I *cannot*.

"How long have you two been married?"

"Five years in December."

"You literally seem like newlyweds," I remark, shamelessly reaching for another cookie to Clara's delight.

They pull up a few wedding pictures, and it looks like something from a fairytale: billowing dresses, windswept curls, and the woods as a backdrop. Their reception was a giant picnic next to a stream, with gingham blankets and mason jars. I'm obsessed with all of the perfect tiny details.

"It's gorge. I love an outdoor wedding," I gush, too embarrassed to admit I've curated a Pinterest board for an outdoor fairytale wedding since my teenaged years.

"You think your monster-hunt with Chris was bad?" Rosie drops her head in her hands. "My brother rallied the entire bridal party to search the area before we chose a location."

With Moth's general distaste for people, I wouldn't have expected him to be a wedding crasher.

"Have you ever … seen anything?" The question slips out before I can stop myself.

"There was this one time," Clara begins. "Part of me feels like I just made it all up, you know? I was out hiking, and I lost track of time. Suddenly, it was pitch-black. Long story short, I end up stumbling into a coyote's den. We don't have many of them here, but I should have been more careful. This creature with red eyes appeared and the coyote just ran off. I ran home as fast as I could." She tells the story all in one breath with her eyes squeezed shut.

"Since then, I've seen shadows. Nothing ever feels unkind. But I do believe that there's something out there. I like to pretend it's some kind of spirit watching over the animals—and us." A serene smile brightens her face before she opens her eyes. "Chris, however, tells a *very different* tale."

"I think he looks for the 'monster' every time he goes hunting," Rosie interjects. "Glad he doesn't have a taste for vengeance."

Vengeance—what does he have to avenge? I just assumed he was an eccentric cryptid hunter. Is it something more personal?

"Honestly, though!" Rosie begins before I have a chance to ask. "You have nothing to worry about."

"As if I'm scared of the forest monster," I chuckle, unable to resist the urge to make my own private joke.

"Have you ever thought about getting a dog like Georgia?" Clara ruffles her hands through their Pitbull mix's short fur.

"Yes! Wouldn't you feel so much safer with a pupper around the house?" Rosie's eyes brighten with possibility. "We could all go to the shelter together this weekend!"

"And then out to brunch?" Clara asks, waggling her dark eyebrows at me.

"I do love brunch." And honestly, a dog would be nice company. After all, Moth isn't going to be around forever. Before I can get the next sentence out of my mouth, Rosie has the website of the nearest shelter pulled up on her phone, while Clara and I to figure out how far we'd need to road trip to go to a drag brunch.

As hesitant as I was feeling about new friendships, the more we talk, the more I feel like we were all destined to meet. But there are a lot of details about my life—both past and present—that I don't think I can share. When it comes to adopting a dog, well, I'll have to figure out how to get one creature off my couch before adding another one. I tell them I'll think about it while Georgia plops her head on my lap and wags her tail.

They're all working together to make a very compelling case.

"Did you want to help us feed the animals? I'm sure they'd love to meet a new friend."

"Ah, that's okay. I should really get going." I think about Moth all alone in the house. I'm sure he doesn't mind that I'm out, but I've gotten so used to life with just the two of us that I weirdly miss him.

"Yeah, Rosie, don't try to put our guest to work!" Clara teases, throwing her arm around her wife.

"Next time!" I promise, leaving with a cookie-filled stomach and an extreme case of puppy fever. I hope Moth is okay— and that he hasn't snacked on any more of my linens. Breathing in the crisp air, I trek down the long dirt driveway to my car.

"Well, hey." I hear Chris's voice before I see him. To my horror, he's leaning against my car, blocking the driver's side door.

Great.

"Oh, hey."

"You're here." His voice is breathy with surprise. My presence is clearly not unwelcome. I was worried that if we ran into each other, it might be awkward. With the way his lips are curling into a smile, it still might be, for me at the very least.

"Yeah, I was hanging out with Rosie and Clara. It was a super last-minute invitation."

"And here I was hoping you had some new information," he croons, as charming as ever.

"No, nothing unusual happening back at my place. I think you can stop worrying." The words come out a little more forceful than I mean them to.

"Stop worrying about my favorite city-girl? Never." He winks. It might be charming if he wasn't blocking the driver's side of my car. "Can I show you something?"

"I'm kind of in a hurry."

"Come on. From one senior monster hunter to the newest junior member." He smiles, nudging my arm. "Don't you want to know more about the thing you saw in the shadows?

Yes.

Yes. I do.

I don't respond out loud, but he must know my answer with the way his eyes light up.

"Follow me."

14.

CHRIS LEADS ME OUT TO AN OLD BARN ON the property. I can't tell what it used to be. It's too large to be a shed; maybe a stable?

"So, is this like your clubhouse?" I ask, stepping into the dim, oversized barn.

"It's our *base*." He sighs.

So yes, it's absolutely a clubhouse.

There are bulletin boards with newspaper clippings and blurry photos on the walls. Articles printed from shady websites, all nested together as evidence. I catch the shape of dark wings spotted with yellow silhouetted in the night sky.

Moth.

Chris's lair is the physical manifestation of a gossip blog. Blurry photographs of the edge of his wings, the glow of his eyes. Poor Moth has paparazzi following him everywhere.

"Clara said she sees him as a sort of guardian," I say, trying to take in all of the details. It doesn't feel like I should be seeing this.

"MOTHMAN CHASES
COUPLE IN A CAR."

"MOTHMAN SIGHTED
AS CROPS BURN."

"LOCALS SUSPECT
MOTHMAN RESPONSIBLE
FOR MISSING CATTLE."

Moth … man.

Wait…

No.

Moth is just a giant man with enormous wings that just happens to look—and when he's in that other form, he's–he's–

Oh.

I have a crush on Mothman.

Literal. Actual. *Mothman.*

This—no—there's no way.

I'm tempted to look around the barn for hidden cameras, but I can't tear myself away from the articles. There's an old photo of the hood of a car, deep claw marks indenting the metal. The sight of it makes my blood run cold. There's no question that Moth could do something like that, but *would* he?

14.

"Mothman…?"

There are sightings of him everywhere. Chasing down cars and leaving deep scratches on the roofs. Looming around the sites of various tragedies; some witnesses even suggest he's responsible. I honestly feel for him. Not only are the headlines dire, but the photos are all blurry and extremely unflattering. *#relatable*

"I personally can't stand the name. You should see the way so-called cryptid enthusiasts jump over hoops to personify this *thing*." He jams his hands in his pockets, pacing the length of the small barn. I can't help but think he's referring to his old friends from high school. "Some of them practically swoon. It's disgusting."

"Swoon. Oh, uh. No way," I choke out. Coming here was probably a bad idea.

Still, I'm enraptured by every wild speculation. Moth is a puzzle I've been trying to figure out since I met him, but doing it like this doesn't seem right. To the writers of these articles, he's a thing that goes bump in the night; they've never seen him polish off a package of cookies or drink a cup of overly sweetened tea. They call him a Harbinger of Death. Though, considering all of the hateful things I've been called online, it could be so much worse.

The idea of Moth being that far out of the woods is strange enough—but all these rumors and sightings? It ties my stomach in knots.

"Clara doesn't know what she's talking about." Chris's voice pulls me from my thoughts. "She's just a wannabe witch who's never actually seen the monster. She has no interest in the facts."

For the first time, I realize there are weapons strung on the walls—big ugly guns are displayed like cherished vintage dishware in a grandmother's home.

All this research.

All this dedication.

It begs the question.

"Why exactly are you looking for this 'monster'?" I don't mean to use air quotes, but my hands hover sarcastically in the air before I can stop myself. Moth is the least *monstrous* creature I've ever met. He's clueless, yet wise: a contradiction with broken wings draped over an antique sofa. All I want is to get back home to him.

"Like, I get the pictures and the curiosity, but—"

"Let me show you something." Chris fumbles with the buttons of his shirt. I guess it's been a while since I've had a make out sesh, but uh, considering the setting and suitor? No, thanks. Besides, whether I want to or not, I have my eyes on someone else.

"Oh wow, I'm flattered, but uh—this isn't really the place," I begin, not sure what to say. How am I supposed to get out of here without offending him?

As I inch out of the barn, my platforms catch on the gravel. If I knew I was going to be in this situation, I'd have worn my glittery work boots.

"Ugh, no—God, no. Not here." He chuckles as if sharing a private joke before giving me a smug grin. "I get that this sort of thing can be a turn on but let me take you out to dinner first, alright?"

Okay, rude. First, the thing about Clara being a "wannabe witch" and now this. I should tell him I'm seeing someone, but the words dry up when he slips his flannel off to reveal a row of pink scars decorating a chiseled chest. They look like they're from a row of claws.

They look like the same ones I had on my wrist—only worse.

"Who did that to you?"

"Who do you think?"

"Why would—" I cut myself off before I can say anything else. Moth can—and has—hurt me. It was an accident, but it still happened. Chris has the same scars across his body. As if in a trance, I gravitate back to the bulletin board of newspaper clippings. I trace a blurry photo of Moth with my fingertips. The gleaming red eyes of a predator stare back at me.

The man in these headlines who terrorized unsuspecting people and the one draped in my living room are somehow the same. It's not as if I haven't thought about him with his teeth bared and hunger in his eyes. I've been thinking about it more and more lately.

I imagine his claws trailing down the small of my back, leaving raised pink marks across my skin. I flush at the thought of his fangs digging just a little too hard in that tender space between my neck and shoulder. What would it feel like to be wanted by him? To be bitten and kissed and clawed until there was no question that I'm his?

His.

With a shaky breath, I swallow the misplaced desire. Is that really what I want?

"Listen," Chris warns, "I know I come on kind of strong, but I care about you, okay?" He places his hand firmly on my shoulder. It takes everything I have to keep a pleasantly natural expression on my face. "If you see those red eyes watching you from the woods, you run. You run as far as you can, and you call me, okay?"

"Yeah, sure thing."

I gulp, eyeing the guns in the corner of the room. What would he do if he found out the "creature" was asleep on my couch? I know the answer to that question, but I don't want to think about it. I make every effort to be as nonsuspicious as possible: I fake interest, I flirt, I silently vow to never let Chris discover the secret I'm keeping, and most importantly, I get the hell out of there.

No amount of lo-fi can stop my heart from racing as I speed home to my monster in the woods.

What was he thinking? Was Moth really trying to hurt them or was he just an old man shouting at kids to get off his lawn? I've felt the two of us growing closer the last few days. As gruff and unfriendly as he can be, I have a hard time imagining he'd hurt anyone.

On purpose, at least.

"I'm home!" I call. The living room glows with the light of dozens of candles. "What is all this?" I ask. A platter with cheese and fruit adorns the center of the set table.

"You were gone for quite a while," Moth responds with a slight shrug. How much effort does he put in to try to sound indifferent?

"I guess I was worried for no reason," I say, more to myself than to him.

14.

His feathery antennae flops forward and then back as if confused by my statement. "You were worried for me?"

If Moth had landed on any other roof—Chris's for example—would he have even survived the night? My stomach twists into a knot, and I lower myself onto the couch.

"Heather?" Moth's fingers comb across my jaw until I look up into his eyes. "Has something happened?"

"What is it that you do out here in the woods?" I finally ask. "Have you ever—you—"

His eyes are gentle, but when his claws gently stroke the length of my arm, I flinch. "It's nothing!" I exclaim, making a beeline for the beautifully set table. I quickly plaster my most award-winning smile on my face. The one that my mom always falls for, and Chris so easily fell for. "Thank you—wow, this, you didn't have to do all this."

"You are afraid." Moth's tone wavers from its usual gruff indifference into something—odd. Broken.

"Not of you." The reply comes before I have to a chance to think. Of course I'm afraid of him, but not for the reason he might think.

Moth stands frozen in the living room, unwilling to take a step closer. If he read some of the exaggerated gossip blogs about me, I wonder if he'd look at me differently—the same way I'm probably looking at him right now.

"Then you are a fool," he says, taking a step away from me. I'm not sure if his flexed claws are a threat or a reminder.

"Okay, first of all, that's rude, and no–no, it was just a weird day."

The real truth is looking across the house at Moth, his red eyes bright and his sharp claws gleaming in the light, all I can think about is how goofy he looked with half my tablecloth hanging out of his mouth. How can someone so menacing look that adorable? I don't know what happened between him and Chris. Maybe it wasn't even Moth that did that. This could all be some misunderstanding. Still, if Chris had his way, Moth would be stuffed and mounted on his wall.

No, I *won't* let that happen. As long as I'm here, he's going to be protected.

A chill pours through the open window and I cross my arms tightly over my shoulders.

"Have you just now realized," he whispers in a low and dangerous voice, "that you have invited a monster into your home?"

The surface of his skin stretches as if the bones are trying to force themselves outward. The fangs I've grown used to seeing poke out from beyond his full lips sharpen into a beak. His face pops and cracks. The sound of it all happening is almost as chilling as watching his transformation unfold. His dark curls melt into equally soft-looking downy feathers. Finally, his eyes become large and owlish.

Just like that the creature from the woods is close enough to kiss. My breath catches when I realize that's something I want, even when he's in this form. Mothman … I want to kiss *Mothman.* The low growl he emits makes me shudder. There's more than fear stirring in my veins, and I shuffle back until the coffee table takes space between our bodies. I gulp, attempting to averting my eyes from his well-sculpted body. A monster—*right.*

A legend.

A cryptid.

In the glow of the candlelight, maybe I *have* forgotten.

"I didn't realize monsters could set up such romantic dates," I say, unable to hide the grin on my face. Candlelight flickers off his body like starlight reflected in a lake. Despite trying to keep my distance, we drift together as if riding some imaginary tide. Here, in this living room, with the food and the candles and the sullen look in his ruby eyes—he's created magic.

"A *date.*" Moth's owlish eyes blink as he mulls over the word. "Even in this form?"

"I mean, I dragged you into my house, didn't I?" I tilt my head up to meet his gaze. Time stands still for a long moment. My breath hitches when his hand encompasses mine, his grip light as if asking for permission.

"So, you did." Moth looks at me as if he's seeing me for the first time. Maybe he is. I straighten my posture, doing my best to not shy away from the look he's giving me. It's not lust or wanting—no, it's something else entirely, something I can't seem to place. *"So, you did,"* he repeats quietly. I hope he finally realizes that I see him too.

I HATE HOW MUCH I LIKE THIS HOUSE WITH Moth in it.

Dangerous? Probably.

Infuriating? Absolutely.

But as strange as this all is, this house has become a home with him standing next to me.

I can't deny how wanted he is, and it's not just his company. It's not just the mornings when the light catches his toned muscles, flecked with gold. It's the way his cheek creases into a dimple when he smiles, the way his claws click on the tabletop as he stares out the window. I've caught myself staring at him more times than I'd like to admit.

The minute his wings work, he's going to leave. He has wanderlust; I can tell by the way his wings twitch as he stares out the window. It's great that the woods are singing to him, but couldn't we press mute for a little while longer? I know he's not some stray cat who can stay cuddled at my side forever, but something has felt different these last few days.

Every lousy headline about him bounces out of my head while I watch Moth flit around the house. He opens each of the cabin windows in a tizzy, which is fair considering the kitchen is filled with smoke.

"I'm usually a great baker!" I shout, fanning the smoke toward the window. "It's got to be this oven."

I toss the cookie sheet down onto the stovetop. One of the brick-hard chocolate chip tahini cookies falls onto the counter with a loud thud.

"I would prefer if you didn't set the entire forest on fire," Moth grumbles, running a clawed hand through his dark hair.

"It's the oven!" I playfully shove at his side. "And it wasn't even a fire, okay?"

He raises an eyebrow, plucking a cookie from the cookie sheet. He turns it over in his claws, inspecting the charred baked good.

"Okay, it wasn't a *big* fire." I snatch it away from him before he can take a bite. I collect the rest and toss them in the garbage. "This batch does *not* count, okay?" Ugh, it sucks to waste ingredients like this. That was the last of my tahini, and it's not like the general store will have any.

"I just wanted to do something to say thank you to Rosie and Clara." I pout, feeling pressure build up in my chest. When you make someone a gift, it's got to be perfect—or, at least, "imperfectly perfect." Mom's great at it. She crafts things that look effortless, leaving just enough little quirks to make sure it looks home-made. I don't have half her presence, charm, nor her wit, but I thought I could do this. "They're the nicest people I've met since moving to this place!"

"This isn't a place for humans," Moth insists. I might be imagining it, but he suddenly seems a little sullen. Maybe he snuck one of the burnt cookies while I wasn't looking.

"The indoor plumbing suggests otherwise."

"Just because it was built here doesn't mean it belongs," he counters with an arched brow. I hate that I love how he looks when he makes that face.

"Oh yeah, you seem *really* inconvenienced," I say, giving him a pointed look. He spent the entire morning draped across my bed reading a book, I think he can cool it with the whole superior forest creature thing. "I just really want them to like me."

"It is the thought that counts, is it not?"

"I don't think those convey any sort of feeling that's worth sharing." I groan, pointing to the trash. The corner of his mouth quirks upward; at least one of us finds this amusing.

After the kitchen has aired out, I go through the rest of my ingredients. I could maybe throw some cookie bars together, but they're going to be basic as hell.

"I don't think I remember how to make friends." I pace, throwing my hands in the air. "I met all the people I knew at networking events. When you boil it down, most of us were coworkers. Everyone I really, really clicked with moved away. Sure, and like sure, we keep in touch when we can, but it's just not the same.

You know, especially with this whole digital detox I am going for?"

Moth blinks.

"You understood like half of what I said, didn't you?" I ask.

"That is a generous estimate." He sighs down at me, tapping his index finger to his chest. "It must be a gift?"

"It *must*," I echo, borrowing his regal tone and earning a glare in the process. How can something as annoying as a glare be so cute?

"Would you accompany me deeper into the woods?" he asks, extending a hand to meet mine. Of course, with a voice like that, I think I'd follow him anywhere. Considering who he is—*what* he is—that probably isn't a good thing. Still, I can't keep the grin off my face. Deeper into the woods, huh?

"I'll get my picnic basket."

Having spent most of my life in Orlando or L.A, I'm not used to seasons. So maybe that's why it feels like magic every time the scent of autumn hits my nose. Leaves in red and orange have fallen into soft piles, obscuring any sign of a path, but Moth walks with confidence. I follow.

It's something else to see him out here in nature. The woods respond to him like an old friend. I watch a squirrel climb him like a tree until it sits upon his broad shoulder like a parrot. The urge to bust out my camera has never been stronger.

I loop my arm in Moth's as we walk; he guides us with ease through the shade of the trees. "Aren't you worried about someone seeing us?" I ask.

"The birds are tweeting their disapproval as we speak." There's a smile on his lips.

"I've had enough mean tweets for a lifetime, thank you." As expected, the joke flies right over his head. He stares through me as if waiting for a punchline. "I meant like, you know, random people seeing us out here."

Chris. I mean Chris. The image of him staring at Moth through the barrel of a gun makes me shiver. Though right now, apart from the wings, he's not recognizable as the "monster" Chris knows him as.

"Humans typically do not wander this far after nightfall." He quirks his eyebrow at me. Again, I'm taken back to the night he chased me through the darkness. Even though he's standing here next to me, it still feels like a strange dream. I gulp.

"What can I say? I like to make an entrance. Wait, do the birds seriously really not like me?"

"The birds think you are fine."

"Good." I pull him closer as we trudge onward. "I'd hate for you to be out of a job."

"I also think you are…" He pauses, as if unable to finish the sentence.

Unfortunately, even now, I think I might be starting to like him enough for the two of us. Once his wing is healed, he'll leave and forget all about me, and this will all feel like some surreal dream. I hold tight to his arm. If it's going to come to an end, I want to enjoy every minute of it, gossip articles be damned.

15.

"So, where exactly are you taking me?"

"May I?" He stands behind me, his hands poised to cover my eyes; he waits until I nod before I feel his fingers on my skin. Gently, he leads me blindfolded toward what I'm guessing is a clearing up ahead.

When he removes his hands, we're at the edge of a field of flowers. They sprawl for what seems like forever; in the moonlight, the gemstone-colored petals almost appear to be glowing. It's like looking at an oil painting.

"Does this please you?" he asks, in a voice so soft and tender I'm weak in the knees.

"It's wonderful."

"Are you tired from the walk? Your legs—they are … short."

I gape at him. What kind of comment was that? By his standards, anyone's legs would be *short.*

"I'm a little tired," I admit, letting my head fall back. We lie together in the field, surrounded by garden mums and canna lilies. For a giant monster who's spent most of his time in the middle of nowhere, Moth knows a lot about flowers. I nearly fall asleep listening to his deep voice as he waxes poetic about the scent of sweet alyssum. Under his gleaming fangs and sharp claws, he's not only a total goof—he's romantic too.

If he hadn't just put his foot in his mouth, it would be a picture-perfect moment for two people who have had enough of cameras for a lifetime.

"If my wing was healed, I would have flown."

"And left me to walk with these stubby legs?" I laugh. "Thanks a lot."

"I would have flown with you."

Oh.

The only time we've flown together, I was too terrified to enjoy the feeling of soaring through the air.

"Why did you save me if you hate humans so much? Don't get me wrong: I appreciate you not letting me plummet to my death, but—"

He shifts his gaze toward me. "Even in a patch of weeds, sometimes a flower blooms. I would rather pluck the fairest blossom from the ground than see her get trampled. It is nothing more than that."

Blood rushes to my cheeks, dizzying me for just a moment. Words like that should be written in cursive script over a sunset photo—a sort of inspirational meme. Even if they might be a little insulting to the rest of humankind.

His gaze doesn't waver. It's spoken like a fact. Heat rises to my face.

"And here I thought I was your witch."

"I am beginning to believe you are no witch at all."

His lips look impossibly soft as they curl into a teasing smile. I swallow hard, my every thought consumed by the idea of my lips on his, heavy breathing, our bodies close. There's so much about Moth that I don't understand, and I'm still not sure how to ask about it. The one thing that I won't question is how safe I feel lying here next to him.

I distract myself by picking flowers in deep purple and white hues. I carefully weave them into a wreath for Rosie and Clara while Moth lounges in the moonlight.

15.

I build up sticks to use as the frame before covering it in the prettiest flowers I can find. It feels good to be working with my hands again; time slips away until I have something I'm proud of.

I twist a few of the black and red flowers together into a chain and place it on Moth's head. The red garden mums match his eyes, and the gothic colors suit him. A smile tugs on my lips as I imagine the way he'd look fully transformed, covered in delicate flowers—that is, until the headlines from Chris's newspaper clippings spring to mind. Moth's claws comb a stray hair from my brow, and I flinch at the sudden contact.

"I wish you would tell me what troubles you."

There's no use beating around the bush about this. I like Moth too much to keep lying. Besides, his observant nature is making it impossible to hide that something is bothering me.

"Someone showed me … stuff about you."

"Stuff?" he echoes dryly, his fang-filled mouth hanging open in a scowl.

"About you like … I don't know." I bury my face in my hands. This is so ridiculous. How would I feel if Moth suddenly approached me with my laptop in-hand, a bunch of tabs open to gossip guru articles about @HoneyBeaLatte?

I'd hate it. But what was I supposed to do? It's like someone showing you a Google search of a match before you're about to go on a date. Of course, I looked! I read every horrifying detail I could at Chris's clubhouse, and those headlines definitely made it to my search bar on a few sleepless nights.

The giant winged creature.

Red bug-eyed monster.

Mothman.

Moth. My Moth.

He has more conspiracy theories and gossip articles online than I do, and that's saying a lot.

I hope what I'm about to ask doesn't make him hate me.

"Have you ever clawed up a car?"

Moth snorts, the sound uncharacteristically awkward. *"Oh."* His voice is surprisingly light. *"That."*

"Wait, so it's true?" I can't imagine him chasing unsuspecting drivers down old country roads, viciously snatching them up in his talons. Did he savor the screams?

"I was not aware people resided in them."

"How?!"

"When you suddenly awaken in a strange place, with no memories and an iron beast is rushing toward you—"

"Wait." I prop myself up on my elbows "You don't remember anything?"

"I woke to a world knowing only it was not mine." His mouth is drawn in a severe line. That sounds so *lonely.* I can't blame him for being confused or even lashing out.

"At least you didn't mean to hurt anyone."

"That…" He stares off, the light in his eyes suddenly dim. "That is not what I said."

"Oh."

His claws trail down the length of my jaw. "You forget what I am."

His touch is gentle, and though the tone he's using is a crisp bite in the night air, neither of us move from each other's arms.

"You don't even know what you are." I angle myself to look at him, really look at him. In the moonlight, he glows like marble. His large body sprawls next to mine; flowers spill from his dark hair and onto our shared blanket, which he's taking up the most of. "Sorry, I didn't mean that. That sounded—"

"It is not incorrect." His gaze is suddenly unfocused and far away. "Long ago, I stumbled into a town, unaware of my differences… it did not go well."

"Why not?" I rest my head on his shoulder, glad he's accepted me using him as a giant pillow at my convenience.

"Have you forgotten those headlines so soon?" He tips his head to the sky, letting out a long sigh, but keeps me close "Too many people know me; they try to find me in the shadows."

I can understand that.

"But it doesn't bother you? Not knowing, I mean."

"Should it?" He pauses as if unsure of how I'll respond, but what strikes me is that it seems like he cares. I don't have an answer for him, but I feel like being void of all memories—even the bad ones—has to be lonely.

"The guy who showed me this stuff—he said you hurt him." I gulp, letting my fingers trail across my chest where Chris had his scar. "He showed me your claw marks on his skin. My other friend, Clara, she said you saved her while she was hiking. She thinks you're some kind of guardian."

"I suspect both are true." Moth sits as stiff as a tree while a squirrel—the same one from before, I suspect—climbs back onto his free shoulder.

"I do not like drunken humans traipsing around my home." With a blunted claw, he scratches under the squirrel's neck. The small animal nuzzles him affectionately. Somehow, I find myself a little jealous "Most of the creatures here feel the same."

I don't know that I can approve of attacking people for partying in the woods, but the way he's snuggling this tiny squirrel reminds me of how mad my mom would get over people scaring our dogs with fireworks on Fourth of July.

This isn't just about him.

"What about *you*?" Suddenly, he shifts his focus back to me. "You disappeared into these woods for a reason. What brought on this 'digital detox,' as you called it?"

I groan, rising from my place on his shoulder, and take my phone from my pocket. I type my username and slide the device into Moth's clawed hands. I've spent the last few nights reading about him. It's only fair I let him do the same.

His dark brow furrows as his ruby eyes scan through the pages. His scrolls, and to his credit, he only asks me a handful of tech-related questions. He swipes and smirks, his eyebrows raising intermittently. He laughs. God, he's cute when he laughs. When I peek over his shoulder, there's a candid photo of me wearing a unicorn onesie at the grocery store, a giant package of toilet paper under my arm.

"I now see how this object could cause you such distress," he grumbles with a furrowed brow. "The things that are written are…" Moth trails off, clearly nervous about hurting my feelings. He must not realize that I've seen and heard it all.

"Yeah. I just don't have the strength to get rid of it, you know?"

"Ah." He nods thoughtfully as if making a decision. He takes the small device in his grasp and crushes it into powder, electric sparks pouring from his palm. "Now it is gone."

Moth looks smug as if he just did me a small favor, like opening a jar of pickles or grabbing a book off of a high shelf, and in a way maybe he has me speechless—and the terrible thing is he has no idea what he did wrong.

"I can't believe you just did that," I gasp, gaping as the dust particles that used to be my phone catch the breeze.

"It was nothing." He grins at me, his ruby eyes squinting into half-moons. I don't think I've ever seen him this amused before. "You seem to be the object of much speculation."

"Says the man who has an entire statue in Point Pleasant," I counter, which wipes the smile off his face.

"You—"

"I mean, I think they got you all wrong, personally." I shrug. "You're way better looking."

This, for whatever reason, makes him laugh—really laugh.

I shake my head. I don't know what Moth is or where he came from, but somehow, he ended up here, next to me, and I'm grateful. I tear my eyes away from his bare chest, reaching for my cup of tea. If I don't do something with my hands, I'm going to reach out and touch him.

Honestly, I'm not sure if now is the right time. Despite everything, who knows what he wants—even if all I can think about is those lips on mine.

"I guess we ended up here for the same reason." I force myself to look away from him. "The feeling of being watched is too much sometimes, right? People called me paranoid, but then someone would post a picture of me dressed up like a goober at Walmart or being stood up on a date..."

"I cannot relate to those circumstances, but I have felt that feeling." He pauses, his teeth dimpling his lip. Finally, he nods. "I am sorry."

"I'm sorry, too." I think of the way I went looking for him with Chris. I, of all people, should have known better.

I raise my teacup to my lips, taking a long sip. The taste is more herbal than I'm expecting—sweet, almost too sweet. I don't remember it tasting this way. Oh, wait … I'm drinking his tea.

"Sorry!" I shove it into his hands. I don't know why it feels so awkward; we're not in middle school or something. But when I look down at the cup, all I can think of is that my lips touched where his have been. God, I wish they would touch me.

"Why?"

His finger tucks under my chin, lifting my face until our eyes meet. His claw trails from my chin up to my cheek before pushing the teacup back into my hands.

"Drink," he commands gently. I tip the mug to my lips, overtaken by the sweetness of honey and the gentle herbal flavors.

I take a slow, hesitant sip.

He takes my mug in his hands and takes a long, measured sip. His red eyes crinkle into what I think might be a smile; our eyes stay locked on each other.

"You like sweet things, don't you?" I ask, wishing I didn't sound so awkward.

His eyes steal a glimpse into my soul. "Yes." There's a smirk on his face; I don't think he's talking about the tea anymore.

Our bodies are suddenly closer; I inhale his scent of oak and moss. Emboldened by the spark in his eyes, I comb through his tangled curls with my fingertips. His feather-like antennae brush against my skin.

His hands seize my waist, pulling me in. He closes the distance between our bodies so there is not an inch between us. We are nose-to-nose, and our breath entangles.

"I can think of nothing sweeter," he rasps. The pressure of his forehead resting against mine sends sparks of anticipation across my skin.

Our lips meet, desperate and slow. He cradles my neck, pulling me closer until my body feels like liquid against his. Goosebumps rise in the wake of his roaming touch, leaving me gasping every time our lips break apart. He uses his claws, carefully trailing up the back of my neck and massaging my scalp. Everything from our bed of flowers to Moth's soft touch is gentle and sweet, I catch his bottom lip between my teeth, biting down and dragging a deep moan from his lips.

I wonder what other sounds I can cause him to make. We kiss until the moon is low, and my body itches to be even closer to his. He pulls me to his chest, restraining himself from going any further. I smirk. Between the two of us, who would have guessed he'd be the one wanting to slow down?

"Wow," I breathe, relaxing into him as I catch my breath.

He plants a firm kiss on my forehead, snuggling close as if we were in our own bed. Despite our difference in size, I'm amazed at how well we fit next to each other; more than that, I can't believe the feelings I've been trying to suppress aren't just one-sided.

I'm in love with Mothman.

And I think he might love me right back.

16.

FOR THE LAST FEW DAYS, IT'S FELT LIKE we were the only two people in the world. Despite Chris's warning, I love Moth—and more than that, I trust him.

We steal kisses in quiet moments. His arms wrap around my waist in the kitchen. We sit together on the small loveseat and watch old movies. Moth complains about the plots being unrealistic. It's all just foolish humans doing foolish human things. Except, he keeps his body pressed against mine, making me wonder if maybe he's the foolish one. Our days together are soft and sweeter than the fluffiest cupcake in a bakery. But when his body presses against mine, I crave something *decadent.*

The thought of Moth tearing off my clothes and taking me on the cabin floor has played through my head so many times that I've started wearing my least favorite dresses around the house, on the off chance he can read my thoughts after all.

Neither of us has said the words, but with each touch and tender kiss, I know he loves me too. The color has come back to his face, and each day, he seems better than the last. I should be happy, but it's bittersweet. I don't want this to end before it has a chance to begin.

I'm heading out to the General Store to pick up a few things for the week. All that we have left in the house are instant noodles, and the sodium is making me break out. It would be nice to get something sweet for Moth, although lately, it's felt like kisses might sustain him alone. We should probably eat real food, I guess.

As blissful as this time has been, I feel bad that he's been so cooped up. It must be hard not being able to soar through the sky. The least I can do is get some fun treats for our next movie marathon.

The General Store is surprisingly busy. Between rushes of customers picking up their weekly special orders, I manage to deliver my gift to Rosie. After that evening with Moth, I remade the wreath for obvious reasons.

"Flowers…" Rosie tilts her head, studying my arrangement.

"For both you and Clara!" I hold it up proudly.

"You know we're not like … looking for a third, right?"

"They are *friendship* flowers."

"I know Clara's cookies were good and all. I get wanting to propose the minute you see her—*I* did."

"It's not—I, ah!" I flush next to the register.

"Relax." Rosie's mouth quirks into a smooth smile. "I'm sure Clara will like your very platonic flowers. They're gorgeous, but for now…" She hangs them on the door next to the welcome sign. "There! This was very sweet of you. Where did you find all of these?"

"Oh, you know … just around." I'm sure Rosie would love the gorgeous little hidden patch of flowers, but I want to keep that place between Moth and I. That night will be another sweet memory I can wrap in little box and tuck it under my bed.

"Well, I love them. Non-romantically."

"I'm never going to live this down, am I?"

"We'll see," she sing-songs as she hops back to the register. "We would love to have you over again."

"I'd like that too." If it's just Rosie and Clara, that is.

As if sensing that he's the last person I want to see in the world, Chris swoops into the shop. This time, he's not alone. He has a batch of flyers under his arm and a crew of five camo-dressed men filing in behind him. They're loud. Like a bunch of dudes who just came out of a CrossFit class. Though, with the way they're dressed, I'd guess they've been hunting. I suck a breath through my teeth and try my best not to be judgmental, but I just don't understand it.

Rosie cringes when Chris posts a flyer on the bulletin board.

"HUNTING COMPETITION," it reads in bold type.

Ugh. I don't bother to read the fine print. I obviously have no interest.

"Heather! Hey! I'm glad you're here." Chris makes a beeline for me, taking my hand in his. It's way more intimate than I would expect. I can't help but think he's putting on a show for his friends.

"Look. There's this contest coming up, and the old owner of your cabin—sweetest old lady you've ever met—knew her land bordered on the hunting grounds, so we were all hoping that—"

"Oh no, no way." I wave my hands. I am not having them traipse around my property with guns drawn. No, nope, not going to happen.

"Oh, come on! It'll only be for one day." Chris's stare smolders. His pearly whites would be hard to resist if I hadn't recently traded in my preference for perfect teeth for fangs. "You can even tag along with me."

"Yeah, no." I shake my head "Sorry. I'm just … not comfortable with that. I obviously can't stop you from hunting, or whatever, but do it somewhere else."

"Stop us from hunting?" One of his friends pipes up from the back.

I cross my arms over my chest. "Yeah, I mean it's a matter of morals." I inwardly cringe as the words leave my mouth. Starting an argument was not my intention. I can tell I messed up as their eyes narrow.

"So, you think you're *like so* much better than anyone who hunts?" Chris mocks the way I speak, earning a laugh from the group. It's a sharp change from the sweet, attentive guy I'm used to interacting with.

I flush. The truth is that I have had hunting on my mind lately—just not the kind Chris and his friends are discussing. Twice in the last week, I've woken up in a cold sweat at the memory of Moth chasing me through the woods, his claws digging into my waist, his fangs at my throat, and his hot mouth on mine. In this dream, I'm not the least bit afraid. I *want* to be his prey—but that's neither here nor there when it comes this conversation.

I shake myself back into the moment, hoping the flush on my face looks like I'm embarrassed by this ridiculous argument.

"What about feeding our families?" Another one of Chris's friends pipes up.

"I'm sorry. Aren't we were talking about some contest or something?" I get that eating meat is a personal choice. Not everyone can afford a vegan or vegetarian lifestyle in a healthy way. I'm not trying to argue that.

"The idea of killing something for fun is just gross." I wrinkle my nose, not making any attempt to hide my disgust. They're already mad, might as well double down.

"I mean, it makes sense a cute city girl wouldn't have the stomach for it." Chris doesn't waste a second throwing me under the bus. "But you could at least let us have our fun."

They all laugh, except for Rosie, who keeps her eyes cast down.

"And you can." I stand firm, even though I can feel my knees shaking under me. I'm severely outnumbered in this conversation. "But using my property? Yeah, that's a no from me."

"But maybe next time, get off your high horse before riding into town," Chris snickers, sounding every bit like the trolls I logged offline to get away from.

"She's such an elitist."
"I wish she wouldn't be so pushy."
"She thinks she's so much better than everyone else."
"This girl is so detached from the real world."
"No one wants you here."

Comments swirl around me like ghosts from my past, clouding the room, pulling me into their invisible web.

"Oh, come on, you look like you're going to cry." A frown creeps across Chris's face. "You don't need to be so sensitive. We're all just talking."

"I literally can't with you!" I snap, stomping my heel against the linoleum.

"You realize you started this conversation, right?" He scoffs. "Why don't you come with us, see what it's all about? I bet you'd surprise yourself."

Hasn't he heard a word I said?

"That doesn't appeal to me in the slightest." Oh god. I'm spending too much time with Moth; I'm starting to sound like him. I bite back a sob while the tears well in my eyes.

He seems like he's enjoying not being the butt of the joke.

"Where do you think your meat from the grocery store comes from?" The blonde one comes closer.

"I'm a vegetarian," I answer back coolly.

"Of course, you are." Another scoffs. "Are you done here? You're blocking the register."

Rosie stares down at the counter. She's not going to say a word to defend me, is she? I'm not sure what her dynamic is with these goons, but I'd at least expect an apologetic glance in my direction.

The sting radiates through my chest. I take my bags, keep my head down, and ride my high horse back to the cabin. If I had made any friends, this moment might have made me lose them.

At least there's one person I can count on. I race home, imagining Moth's arms enveloping me, making me feel safe and wanted. The scent of cinnamon and oak tickles my nose as soon as I pass through the threshold, instantly calming me.

"Hey! I picked up these honey cookies. I guess someone from town makes them. They seem like—"

The scarf he had wrapped around his wing is laid out on the bed, and Moth is nowhere to be found.

A flower sits on my pillow.

A thank you, and a goodbye.

And, just like that, this house feels a little less like home.

17.

AS A RULE, I DON'T DRINK.

It hits me too hard and gives me a terrible headache. I feel hungover and puffy for days.

Popping the cork, I don't think about the consequences. At least, not long enough to care. Everyone in town hates me.

And I have a crush on the literal *Mothman*, who left me. So, you know, that's great. Love this for me. *Foolish,* he'd called me. His words burn a gaping hole in my heart.

I pour myself a glass of wine, swishing the dark liquid around in the glass.

The worst thing about it?

He was right all along.

17.

A city girl in the woods? I'm more like a fish in the desert, flopping aimlessly without an ounce of water to revive me.

No grace, no dignity, just arguments in the middle of convenience stores and the feeling of suffocation squeezing my lungs. Moving away didn't fix a damn thing. I was foolish to think it would. What if no one in this town is ever going to like me?

I wanted to connect with who I am outside of the brand I built. I didn't consider that person might actually suck. Since moving out here, have I actually done anything to connect with nature? The weather is perfect tonight, and there's a cool breeze. A real outdoorsy person would make a bonfire, so that's exactly what I'll do.

Okay, it turns out making a fire is way more complicated than I thought. After a few failed attempts rubbing sticks together, I give up and use the starter log I found in the shed. Soon, the fire is roaring, and honestly? It's incredible. Most importantly, it's a good opportunity for s'mores, which I desperately need.

Is it the classiest dessert to go with a bottle of cheap wine? Probably not. Still, I run inside to fetch marshmallows, graham crackers, and most importantly, chocolate. When I go back outside with my bounty, I freeze at the sight of wings barely illuminated by the flames.

He's back.

Why is he back?

I should give him a piece of my mind.

"D'ya want a s'more?" I ask, my words slurring together. I've forgotten that when it comes to getting drunk, I fall into the "overly friendly" category. A glass of wine somehow brings out the hostess in me even if I had hoped it would bring out my rage. I make a mental note to summon it during the rest of our conversation. He's not getting off that easy.

He hangs by the campfire. When I get closer, Moth wrinkles his perfect nose at me.

"Are you trying to burn down our woods?" He crosses his arms. "How foolish are you to leave a fire like this unattended?"

"I was inside for one minute!" My voice shakes. God, I'm sick of getting yelled at.

"Something has happened." He brushes away a tear I didn't realize I'd let fall. How dare he act innocent right now?

I shake my head.

It's fine.

I'm *fine.*

I'm sure the forest monster has bigger things to worry about, but my throat burns with sobs I want to spill onto his chest.

"What do you care?" My body slumps onto one of the fallen logs by the fire. In the dark, there's no way he will notice my eyes shining with tears, right? Right.

"You humans are so fragile." He scoffs, taking a seat next to me, leaning toward the flames.

"I'm *not* fragile!" I scream the words, ignoring how every piece of me feels like it's breaking—and yup, there's the rage I wanted to summon earlier.

17.

"Heather, what is the matter?" Moth tries to touch me, but I shift, already miles away.

"What are you doing back here?"

He blinks at me, tilting his head. "Was I not supposed to return?"

"You left." I shake my head. "The scarf! The flower! Uh, hello? You left me."

"If I had intended on saying goodbye, I would not have left you a Jonquil." There's a glint in his eyes as though he knows a secret.

"I'm sorry for not being well-versed in the language of flowers or whatever!" I shout.

A laugh escapes him. He picks up the bottle of wine next to me and begins to examine the label.

"Do you drink?" I ask, wondering what kind of drunk Mothman would be.

"I do not."

"Me neither," I reply, snatching it from his hands and taking a sip out of the bottle.

"And yet tonight?"

"And yet tonight," I repeat.

His fingers trace along my chin. "Because you thought I would not return?"

"There's more to it than that." I don't want to share what happened. He'd probably think it was silly.

"You are cold," he states, pulling me back from the fire. I guess *maybe* I was standing a little close. I spin to face him and notice his little antennae wiggling in the wind like feathers.

Cute.

He's so cute.

It almost makes me forget how mad I am at him for disappearing. I mean, he could have at least left a note.

"What are you smiling at?" His voice is as dark as night itself.

"Nothing!" I shove at his chest, resisting the urge to burrow my head against his firm body. His familiar smell of oak and moss instantly calms me; I'd sink to the ground without his hands at my waist. This stability is exactly what I wanted to feel when I raced home.

"Your mood is erratic."

I gesture to the wine. "That's kinda the whole point."

"Do you expect me to stay in the house every time you leave?" His wings spread wide. I flinch at the sudden movement—and then I realize.

His wings are better.

He had no reason to come back, but here he is, towering over me, with that look in his eyes. I shrink away from him, perching on the log bench in front of the fire. "Why are you here?"

"Clearly, you cannot be left alone. You know I cannot always be around to save you."

"I know. I get it. I don't belong in your precious woods," I huff, tucking my knees close to my chest.

He takes his place next to me, his large thighs touching mine; the sensation alone is enough to send lightning across my skin. "Why would you think that?"

"Um, hello? *'You should not have come to the forest.'* You literally called me out the first time we met." Normally, my low-toned impression would at least earn a raised eyebrow. Instead, his high-set cheekbones tint in a rosy, pink blush that I'm sure I must be imagining. "I'm just some city girl taking up space."

"*You*—" Before I can process the tenderness of his voice, his hand cups my face just under the chin. "—are a wildflower, vibrant and unpredictable; wherever you choose to settle, roots will follow."

"But you said—"

"I knew if you stayed here, I would not be able to keep myself from you." He strokes the edge of my face with the smooth side of his claws. A shiver ripples through me like a stone tossed into a river. Just when I think the feeling has subsided, his fingers move ever so slightly, and I'm desperate for more of his touch.

"This is not a conversation for now." He eyes the bottle of wine still in my grasp.

"Please…"

"I saw how the sun silhouetted you while you sat up in that tree. Your hair tangled with leaves. The bark of that oak pulled at your billowing skirts as if trying to pull you close."

"I was *foolish*," I say, unable to stop echoing his own words back at him.

"Yes." His lips quirk into a sly grin. "I happen to find your frivolity … intriguing."

My … what?

"If I am your Moth, you are my flame." Then, in a voice as dark as the night sky, he says, "I could not stay away even if I wished it."

"Did you want to stay away?"

"What do you think, my flame?" He dips forward so that our noses touch, his wings unfurling behind him like two flower petals—dark and delicate, just like the sound of his voice.

"I–" I can't breathe, can't finish a single thought, much less a sentence while he's sitting so close.

"You have more questions," he observes.

I raise the wine bottle to my lips, taking a long sip. I study him for a moment. What should I ask? He doesn't remember where he's from. He must have had a family at some point in time. Unless he really was some government experiment, he couldn't have just come from nowhere.

"I'm sorry." I turn my attention to the flames. There's so much I don't know about him. With his memories gone, there's not much he even knows about himself. At Chris's clubhouse, I saw that some of those newspaper clippings dated back to the sixties. Moth has been alone for a long time.

"Why?" His voice doesn't have the solemn tone I'd expect.

"When's your birthday?"

"My what?"

"I don't know your birthday; how will I know when to make you a cake?!" I yell—there's the misplaced rage again.

He squints at me, unsure of what to make of my exclamation.

"What? I'm like a really good baker!" I shove a finger against his chest. "My recipes have been picked up by T.V. networks and blogs. Just because I started that tiny fire once doesn't mean I can't—"

He has no idea what I'm talking about. I take a deep breath to center myself, but it's too late. He's doubled over, his broad shoulders shaking—oh my god, he's laughing at me! And not just a good-natured chuckle with the little sideways smirk I normal get. It's ridiculous, and as infuriating as it is attractive. When he raises his head, there are tears in the corners of his eyes.

It's not that funny!

"I'm being serious!" I huff, which makes the laughter start again.

"You are an amusing drunk."

"Shut up. I'm making s'mores."

He's mean. I'm drunk. We're sitting in front of a campfire. S'mores are long overdue.

Moth looks on with interest as I assemble the first s'more. The marshmallow kisses the flames until its golden brown; it's strangely calming.

"If I was still online, this whole night would be a story. About how I had a bad day and decided to build myself back up." I look at the fire dancing in the night sky. The nearly charred marshmallow catches on fire and falls into the embers.

"By the end of the post, I would have convinced myself to start again, to make something new." I add more marshmallows to both our sticks, instructing him to follow my lead.

"I simply do not understand why people would care so much about watching the life of a human."

"Says the man who's been staring at me through my window since I moved in," I shoot back. He has nothing to say in his defense. When his marshmallow is golden brown, I assemble his s'more and offer it to him. As a lover of sweets, I'm surprised when he doesn't take it right away.

"Well, if you don't want it..." I pull my hand back, but his hands catch mine first.

"It would be rude to deny a gift." He clutches it between his claws.

God, he's such a goof.

The s'more crunches in between his row of fangs; his antennae bobbles.

Marshmallow sticks to his fingers. I watch as his tongue slides down his ring finger; I catch a glimpse of his fangs in the moonlight.

If I kissed him, he'd taste like summer camp.

Moth's dark laugh echoes into the night.

"We have established you can't read thoughts, right?" I ask, sure that the wine has made me sloppy and obvious.

"They are not hard to discern." I'm mesmerized by the length of his dark eyelashes. People pay good money for extensions like that. Hell, *I've* paid good money for extensions like that. How is someone so intimidating allowed to be so soft and glamorous up close? "Why are you not afraid of me?"

"Oh my god. We have covered this." I throw my head back with an exasperated groan. Why does he insist on killing the vibe? "You seriously think I should be afraid of you?"

"Yes." He tightly wraps his arms and wings around me like a blanket. My head falls back onto his chest and once again he's my giant pillow. "Why are you not?"

I want to tell him something cool, like "I'm not like most," but it would be a flat-out lie. There are a million people in this world just like me. But the way he's looking at into my eyes, it feels like I'm the only one that matters to him.

"You're nice." It's too simple of an answer for the moment we're in. He gives me sweeping poetry every time he opens his mouth, and I have the romantic prowess of the back of a cereal box.

"Nice?" His lips crack into a toothy grin. His comforting embrace loosens. "You would choose to be held by a harbinger of death?"

If that's what he is, I'm not afraid. Sometimes death means a new beginning, which I need. His skin radiates no warmth, but I can feel the beat of his heart.

"Yeah," I say, the weight of exhaustion making my eyelids heavy.

"Tell me again when you're not high on sugar and drunk on wine, little flame," Moth whispers in my ear. He scoops me in his arms, cradling my body tight to his chest.

"Can I ask you something else?" Drowsiness threatens to overtake me with every step toward our little cabin in the woods.

Our cabin. My face burns at the thought of the two of us creating a real life here, together.

"Anything, my flame."

God, I love the sound of that.

"Are you wearing pants—like how does—" I lose my train of thought as soon as he barks with laughter.

"A conversation for another day." He barely composes himself to get the sentence out. The way his fangs look when he smiles is just too cute.

"Have I made you uncomfortable?"

"Nah." My brain has accepted his exoskeleton-covered legs as pants, even if he has been technically naked this whole time. It's only weird when I let myself think about it for too long.

"You really think I belong?" The last of my insecurities slips from my lips. In response, he presses a kiss onto my forehead as if whispering a prayer.

"Heather." His voice slides across me like a heavy blanket. "You are home." With those tender words, I'm tucked into bed.

18.

I WAKE WITH MOTH'S WINGS TIGHT AGAINST my skin. I blurted feelings in between sips of wine and bites of toasted marshmallows. I don't remember all of them, but I remember his promise.

His long lashes flutter as he stirs, and his lips curve into a smile. "Good morning," he says, pulling me closer. I nestle my cheek against his chest; I think I've found my new favorite pillow.

He smells like campfire and crisp leaves. I breathe in the scent of outdoorsy scent and feel a smile stretch across my face. "You stayed." I yawn, rubbing the sleep out of my eyes. "Why?"

"You asked." He shouldn't be able to make my heart race with just two words.

He's softened since he first arrived here, but sometimes it feels like I'm pulled close and pushed away. I've been entangled in the web of a fickle spider, playing with his food before he devours me whole. I think I might let him when he looks at me like that.

"Are you alright?" he asks.

"Besides the pounding in my head and the fact I can never go back to the closest store for groceries ever again, fine." I sigh. "I don't want to drive an hour to Walmart, so I guess we'll just starve."

"You will not starve." His eyes linger up and down my body.

Years of internet comments about the size of my body jump to the forefront of my mind.

"Just because I'm not some forest wisp—"

"You will not starve." His arm wraps around my waist, pulling me tight to his chest. "I will not allow it."

Oh.

A smile spreads across my lips. I want to kiss him, but I'm positive my breath smells like sour wine and sugar. Instead, I slip out of bed and freshen up before giving in to temptation.

We let the day slip away in comfortable monotony. I sleep away my hangover while Moth lounges on the loveseat.

If I have to cook another meal or do another dish, I'm going to scream. As much as I love Moth's little cheese and fruit trays, I need something to soak up the wine-sick feeling in my stomach.

I pull out my phone—at least I try to. It's not in the usual spot because someone turned it into electronic confetti a few days ago.

During my first drive into town, I think I remember passing a diner, right at the edge of the woods.

18.

Unfortunately, I can't google the menu, but I should at least be able to get eggs and hash browns.

I glance at Moth. His nose is buried in a collector's edition of *Emma* by Jane Austen. I watch his ruby eyes flick over the pages; he's relaxed, clearly feeling at home.

He'd almost look human if I put a hat on him to hide those cute bouncing antennae.

Long sleeves, too.

I'll need to dig out a pair of tinted glasses too, and pants—he's definitely going to need pants.

If we were in LA, no one would bat an eye. His hands just look tattooed and very well-manicured. Standing together, we might just look like an eccentric music duo.

"Do you want to go on an adventure?"

"MOTH!" I squeak, yanking the plastic carafe out of his claws. We've been at the diner for five minutes, and he's already pouring maple syrup down his throat.

"Is this not for consumption?" He tilts his head, blissfully unaware of the grossed-out look our server is giving us.

I cover my face with my hands. But of course, the giant man with the hummingbird appetite would draw attention; I shouldn't be surprised. At least he's not eating the tablecloth.

"It's not a drink!" I shake my head, pointing down at the menu. "You pour it on pancakes or waffles. Or whatever."

"I suppose I will order the 'whatever,'" he says thoughtfully.

I open my mouth to correct him when I notice the lopsided grin on his face. He's totally messing with me.

I reach across the table and boop the tip of his nose. He's earned a few stares from patrons, but I can't imagine any of them suspect him to be anything other than some random goth that's stumbled into their town. He's wearing a pair of my stretchiest leggings and a long black poncho, which I usually use as an oversized wearable blanket. He looks far from average with his wings tight against his back, a hat, and a pair of tinted glasses, but he does look human.

That's all we can really ask for in this situation.

"I take back my earlier comment. Humor is a very good look on you," I say before turning my attention to the menu.

A small gluten-free section catches my attention. At a dive in the middle of nowhere like this, it's surprising, but after talking to the server, I learn the owner's grandson has celiac; she wanted to make sure her whole family could gather together and eat breakfast. Which is, like, stupidly adorable. I go for the blueberry pancakes, and Moth goes for the waffles. He orders off the gluten-free menu too, just so we can share. It shouldn't feel like anything special, but it is. The number of times I've had to remind exes of my dietary needs was always frustrating. I've had to coax them to even taste my cooking. With Moth, there's no hesitation. It's nice—no, it's beyond nice.

We drink coffee sweetened with cream and steal bites across the table. Everything is surprisingly delicious. I move to the other side of the table so the two of us can share a little easier, keenly aware of the way our bodies press together every time I move my fork. It feels good to be out with him. Like, we're a normal couple on a normal date.

I look down at the food sprawled across the table. Even in its chaos, it's somehow artfully arranged. I picture it in a square grid with my signature filter to pull out the brightness.

Breakfast for dinner is for winners 😉 #nightowl

My followers would respond with drooling face emojis and unsolicited advice to cut carbs to fix my thyroid. People would write to me about their diner orders, and for a moment, the internet would feel like it was in the room with me, sharing a burnt cup of coffee.

I hate that I miss it. But at least the trolls can't find me here.

A chime drags my attention to the doorway. I stand corrected. Chris waves across the diner as if he wasn't a total jerk to me at the store yesterday. His hunting buddies file in after him, settling into a nearby booth, but Chris doesn't follow suit. Instead, he makes his way toward Moth and me. I force a smile. I do not want to start any drama—especially with Moth next to me.

"You are not pleased," Moth observes.

"Huh?"

"Your nose did not scrunch."

"What?"

"When you smile, you..." He scrunches his nose like a bunny to demonstrate. The hat hiding his antennae shifts ever so slightly on his head. Oh my god. If he wasn't wearing it, they'd be flopping like ears. It's so cute I might die.

There's no way I look even a fraction as adorable when I smile. All the pictures I have of myself smiling are posed. It's a beauty pageant smile, where you lip the word "money" as you look into the camera. There are some snapshots from my childhood where I resemble a mouse, with a broad toothy grin and scrunched nose, just the way Moth had demonstrated. But that was well before Mom taught me how to do my "pretty smile." I didn't know that was a face I could still make.

"They have troubled you?" Moth asks, turning his attention back to Chris. His eyes flicker a brighter shade of red, and I hope to God the sunglasses are enough to hide his darkening expression.

"Yes—no—we got into a fight about their dumb hunting contest."

"You wished to enter?" There's a snarl on the edge of his lip. I nearly gag on my breakfast at the thought of it. Me, holding a weapon, hunting down animals?

"Ew, no," I exhale. "Can you believe they wanted to use the woods around our—my house?" My disgust seems to put him at ease for a moment. Heat rises to my face. Moth doesn't seem to notice that I almost referred to the cabin as ours, and I don't point it out again. Sure, he's been staying with me, but that's just because…

I squeeze his hand gently, reminding myself that I'm not alone. Chris may think I'm just some random city-girl, but I have Moth on my side.

18.

"Heather! Hey!" Chris is upon us. There's a look in his eyes I can't quite place when he looks at Moth. "And...?"

"Ah, this is my friend from LA..." I trail off. Calling Moth well, *"Moth"* seems like a giant red flag.

"Could have guessed that much." Chris laughs. He seems to fixate on the way the darkness of Moth's black claws climbs up his hands, spindling like veins on his shimmering skin. "You guys painting or something?"

"Or *something*." Moth's voice sounds even deeper in comparison to Chris's. His arm loops around me, pulling me tight against his body in an unexpectedly protective gesture. I blush all the way down to my core. He doesn't need to worry so much. It's not like Chris is going to try to hunt me. At the same time, I can't say I mind how warm Moth's body feels next to mine.

"We have a ton of fun projects to do around the cabin," I interject.

"Ah well, when you're finished with all the artsy stuff and have some real work you need to get done, call me," Chris says. God, could he be any more obnoxious?

"Mmm." I open my mouth to make a quip about the frailty of masculinity but stop myself. After our argument yesterday, nothing I say would get through to him. Still, I shouldn't let him talk to Moth like that.

"I'm sure he can't do much with those nails," Chris challenges, as if Moth isn't sitting right next to me.

Moth's hand moves down from my shoulder until it sits comfortably at my waist; he pulls me taut against his body. I shiver as his lips part in a predator's grin. "You would be surprised." He smirks.

Oh my God, he did not just say that. *Act normal. Act normal. Act normal.* But how can I when Moth holds me the way you would a candle you're shielding from a breeze? He's staking his claim.

I'm *his* flame, and he won't let anyone else have me.

The protective energy he's emitting causes desire to build in me. If just the touch of his fingertips on my waist is driving me crazy, what could the rest of him do?

"This has been like *so* nice, but we really should get going," I squeak. God, I need to rein my thoughts back in. I squeeze Moth's hand, and he releases me so that I can slide out of the booth.

He follows, rising to his full seven feet; his hand reclaims its spot at my waist, guiding me to the cash register as if we're making an entrance at a grand ball.

Chris gapes, clearly not expecting Moth to be as tall as a professional basketball player. I feel a little smug with his arm around me. It's not that I want to make Chris jealous. It's just that after all the comments about my shoes and my clothes, it's nice to be next to someone who doesn't care. For all the quips Moth has made about me, they've never been about my appearance. I think he likes the way I glitter.

"I don't suppose you'd want to come on a hunt with us tomorrow? Maybe you can convince our girl to—" Chris stays in step with us, speaking as if I'm not literally right here.

"Heather." Moth lowers himself to whisper in my ear.

"Yes?"

"Why is *it* still speaking?"

A snort-laugh escapes me before I can stop it. I clamp a hand over my mouth to muffle the rest of my laughter, regaining my composure.

"No hunting by my house, and that's final," I say to Chris, who, from the look on his face, I assume, heard everything. "Have a good night, 'kay?"

"Yeah … you too."

"Let's go home," I whisper to Moth, trying to keep the smile off my lips. I tug him toward the door.

Moth's hand doesn't leave the small of my back until we're seated in my breadbox of a car. If I hadn't been standing between them, I think those two would have destroyed each other. "A friendly reminder maybe not to refer to other humans as *it*," I snicker, before flicking on the radio. An old country song by Hank Williams fills the space between us

Moth only grumbles, looking at the road ahead.

He's not the chattiest guy, but he's even quieter than usual on the drive home.

I can't stop thinking about what he said about the *sort of thing* his fingers could do. With the way his jaw is clenched, I think he's still thinking about that bizarre hunting invitation.

"Don't let that asshole get under your skin," I say, but it's no use. Moth just wordlessly stares out the window. I can't figure out what happened. We were literally attached at the hip in the diner, but now smashed together in my tiny car, we feel more distant than ever.

19.

CRAVING WARMTH AND WANTING TO GIVE him space, I draw a bath, throwing in a honey bubble bar I'd been saving for a rainy day. Steam fills the room until the air smells like sweetened tea and cakes. The phantom touch of Moth's hands lingers on my waist as I strip out of my clothing, leaving them in a puddle on the tile.

Things between us felt so good in the diner, but maybe a shared plate of pancakes just breeds fake intimacy. But then there was last night and the way he looked at me in the firelight.

The wine has made the memory hazy, but I remember the look in his eyes—at least, I think I do. God, this is why I don't drink. It makes my inflammation unbearable, sure, but it also makes me overthink every feeling I had while I was drunk.

19.

What was real and what did my desperation project onto the situation? I sink low into the water, pull my knees to my chest, and let my head fall forward. Moving out here was supposed to be simple, and wow, is that the *last* word I would use to describe my life.

After my bath, I wrap myself in a satin robe; with each movement, the fabric clings to my damp body and I wish it was Moth's arms around me instead. When I head into the living room, he's decidedly not looking at me. Of course, he isn't. Sure, we've shared kisses in fields of flowers, and pining looks across firelight—that doesn't mean he wants more.

It doesn't mean he wants me.

When I draw close, his body twitches in a way that confirms that, for whatever reason, his choice to ignore me is deliberate.

"Are you going to tell me what's going on?" I perch on the armrest of the loveseat staring him down.

"It is no matter."

"You have been sulking since we got in the car."

"Heather—"

"Just talk to me!"

"'Our girl.'" The words come in a low growl; his claws uncontrollably spasm. The sight makes my heart thud faster. He draws his hands to his sides in fists. Then, it hits me: this giant powerful winged man is on the cusp of unravelling. *Why*?

"What?" I choke out.

"He called you '*our* girl.'" The desire in his eyes is all-consuming.

"Chris?" I run through the bizarre conversation in my head, trying to remember the moment that Moth is fixated on. Honestly, with all the hyper-masculine tension, and Moth's hands on my waist, the whole interaction is a blur.

My lips curve into a smile. Usually, jealousy is so unattractive to me, but it looks good on him. He's all predator with the soft vulnerability of prey in his ruby eyes. I let him stalk toward me, closing the distance between us. Without touching him, I stand as tall as my tiptoes will allow as he dips down so that we are eye-to-eye.

"Moth—" I murmur, desperately wanting to kiss him. Our lips are close enough to touch. Despite all of the soft stolen kisses, this feels different. Want rises in him with every single moment we're not touching. Moth's jaw tenses. Then, in one swift movement, he pulls me into his lap.

"You are *not* his." His claws glide across my jaw, and I nod, suppressing a moan; I want—no, *need*—to be closer to him.

I'm dizzied by his touch. His thighs are warm beneath mine, thick and strong like the base of a tree. The men I've dated in the past have been built like twigs; this man is a whole forest. I swallow hard. There are three words I've wanted to say to him ever since that first night. Three little words that have absolutely terrified me.

"Make me yours."

And with those three words, the monster of the forest is finally unleashed. His lips press against mine, hungry and firm as if it's the first and the last time he's ever going to be kissed. His arms wrap around me, keeping my waist clutched tight against his body as he rises from the loveseat. He holds me like I'm nothing and kisses me like I'm everything in the world he's ever wanted.

"How do you want me, my flame?" His tongue flicks down my ear, causing warmth to rise in my lower stomach.

I hook my legs around his waist, kissing him harder. I can't think of the words to say, but I seem to get the message across by biting his bottom lip, harder than the first time I tried it. We've kissed before, but nothing like this; each movement is desperate and deliberate. I'm lost in a rush of sensation when I feel him pressed firmly against me. I trail my fingers down the length of his thigh, but he catches my hand in his. A devilish grin hints at the side of his mouth.

"And what will you do if it's too much?" His whispers alone could destroy me. Moth pulls away for just long enough for me to ache.

"Please don't stop," I pant. I've waited so long for this moment. My fingers trail down his abdomen; the wings at his back sprawl out, flitting up until our feet are off the ground.

"What will you do, my flame?" He cups my face, holding it firm. It doesn't matter how hard I strain. I can't move forward and kiss him.

We levitate inches off the floor. My desire for him grows with his wingspan. Moth's laugh is cruel as I struggle to move my lips back to his.

"Patience is something you wanted to work on, was it not?" His lips trail up my neck, hesitating only when he reaches my lips.

"*Moth!*" I groan.

"What will you do?" We're a foot off the ground, his wings are—way too big for this cabin. I spare a single thought for the porcelain poodle collection on the mantle as the figures crash to the ground as a dark hunger pools in his eyes.

"Heather..." he prompts. Right. He asked a question. *What will I do if this is all too much?*

"Oh my god, I'll scream some random word like 'pineapple,' okay?" I let my hands trail down his hips, farther than I'd ever dare to touch. One part of his form has shifted I discover as my finger trail down the length of his cock.

"I will stop the moment you tell me to; you understand?" He pulls away. This is the first time he's truly paused.

Nodding up at him, I hook my hands around his neck. I want this. *I want him.*

"That goes both ways." Whatever games we decide to play tonight, he needs to know we both have the power to pull back if we want to. We've never talked about the sorts of things we like in bed. But I can tell by the quake in his limbs that he's holding back. I like the playful possessiveness he's showing me. The moment I give him permission, he's going to lose control. *I can't wait.*

"Are there provisions to be taken?" His throat bobs. The tension Moth appears to be holding in his jaw alone suggests the restraint he's using is causing him more and more physical distress by the second.

"I have an IUD." Thank God, because even if I did happen to have a stray condom packed away in one of my suitcases, there's no way it would fit him. He's uh—*wow*. My face burns as I consider the logistics of his body and mine together—he's *giant.*

With one *snick* of his claws, Moth begins to tear through the thin satin of my robe. He slices down the fabric in an agonizingly slow movement, his hand lingering on the small of my back before the ruined garment falls away from my body. "I will not hurt you."

"What if I ask you *really* nicely?" I purr in his ear. He raises an eyebrow as a devilish grin spreads across his face. It's embarrassing to admit how much I crave the scratch of his claws and bite of his fangs—but I do.

"Who am I to deny you?" His growl sends tingles down my entire body.

Sharp fangs slide across my neck, nibbling up to my ear then back down to my shoulder.

He bites—hard this time. The pressure of his teeth on my sensitive skin is a delicious blend of pain and pleasure, prying another moan from my lips.

"Yes, *God* yes."

If he holds me any tighter, I'd be crushed—and it still wouldn't be enough.

I want—need—more.

Moth's desire is clear. As our bodies grind together, I feel his hardness against my thigh as his hands explore every part of me, never letting my feet touch the ground.

"Please," I beg, taking hold of his hips, but I'm at the mercy of his slow deliberate touch. Hoisting me up with one hand, he's positioned himself at my opening. Rocking my hips, I attempt close the distance between us, but he holds me at bay, teasing me with the tip of his cock until my vision blurs with want.

The need to feel every inch of him inside me increases with every moment. There's a look of mischief on his face, as if he's enjoying the sight of me squirming with anticipation.

"*Please.*" I claw my nails into his shoulders. We've barely even started and I'm already seeing stars. His whole body quakes with each purposeful movement. Despite his dilated pupils, he's *still* intent on making me beg. I'd be annoyed if I wasn't so damn turned on.

"Please, *what?*" There's an edge to his voice as the two of us drip with desire for each other. There's only one answer I want to give.

"Take me!"

Moth doesn't waste another second; with inhuman speed, he has my back against the wall. With one sharp thrust, he enters my body. I bite down on his shoulder, rocking my hips until his full weight is on top of me. Capturing my bottom lip between his teeth, he nibbles. The prick of his fangs has my whole body on edge. His tongue fills my mouth and our lips lock in a kiss that claims me body and soul. Our bodies shudder against each other's like two windup toys finally let loose. At my demand, his thrusts come at a steady rhythm, faster and faster until I'm screaming his name. A giggle escapes me. I imagined the intensity—but not how *fun* it would be to be with him like this. Pleasure builds with each movement he makes, as if he knows exactly what is going to light the spark inside me.

His wings have a life of their own, as we crash from the wall to the couch to the countertop, various knick-knacks, books, and artwork tumble around us. *Maybe we should have taken this outside.* The thought of us together bathed in moonlight makes a shudder run through me. I wrap my legs around his body, meeting him with each thrust until the sparks turn into a roaring fire. I'm set ablaze by the tender touch of his claws and his firm mouth on mine. I know he can't read my mind, but with the way he grabs, and pulls, and takes everything I give with such pleasure and grace, I'm beginning to wonder. His smiling mouth rests on mine in between kisses—it's not a smirk or a slight pull at his lips. Moth is full on grinning as our bodies meet and it's just *perfect. He's perfect.*

"Heather," he says, with his forehead resting on mine. "You bewitch me." The rumble of his voice pulls me further into bliss.

Bewitch.

It's such a strong word for the captivation I feel as his throat bobs, the tension building between us. His hand greedily climbs up my hips to my waist, holding me tight as he steadies his pace.

"I'm *yours*," I whisper, and he moans at the admission. His heavy, rhythmic thrusts have me biting my lip to keep from screaming. When he begins to pull away, I grasp his shoulder, driving him deeper.

"*Don't* stop."

"Does my little wildflower want more?"

Moth's chuckle is dark but unthreatening. He catches me by both wrists, and with a single hand, he cuffs them above my head, and *oh*—that's good. My name is a murmur—a whisper—a prayer as he buries his lips in my hair.

His fangs nip the edge of my ear, trailing down to my shoulder. This bite is harder, unrestrained, and everything I need. Pressure burns brighter and brighter until the inferno consumes every inch of my skin, with Moth not far behind me. I'm still reeling as his body explodes into mine; being filled with his satisfaction threatens to bring me back over the edge.

Our breath is heavy, and a giddy burst of energy suddenly rushes through me.

"Fuck, that was hot," I blurt out. For a second, I worry what his response will be. Moth is poetic and brooding. He'd never say anything that crass without it being wrapped in poetry.

My creature doesn't bristle or shy away. He just kisses me firmly on the lips.

"Mine." The words are lazy and inelegant with hunger, like he's laying claim to the last croissant in a bakery.

If tonight is anything to go off, I will always be a snack for Moth. Gathering me in his arms, Moth tucks me into his wings, and just like that, I'm home.

It's not like I've never had sex before, but what even was that? I've been lying in bed for God-knows how long, and my limbs feel glued to the mattress. For all the bumping around the cabin we've done tonight, I'm glad we somehow made our way back to bed. I savor the feeling of my soft blankets wrapped around my bare skin. Moth had held me close for a while but got up for some unknown reason a few minutes ago.

Why anyone would leave bed after that is beyond me. I force myself to stretch, already missing the feel of his body next to mine when he reappears to press a glass of water into my hands.

"You are an angel," I say, downing half of it in one shot. I didn't realize how thirsty I'd become until my lips touched the glass.

"Do not let the wings fool you."

"It's not just the wings I'm talking about," I reply, still dizzy with the world-shattering feelings he sent rippling through my body. Before I can say another word, he takes me in his arms, letting the blanket fall from my body. I curl up against him as he carries me to the bathroom. The shower steams with the smell of eucalyptus. He sets me down on the tile, having to slump down so that he can fit in the small space next to me. One hand works shampoo through my tangled hair while the other holds my still-boneless body close to his chest.

"You are extraordinary." He breathes the words as light as air across my damp skin. I melt further into him. I don't know what it is—his words, his touch, small gestures—but I feel safety like I've never felt before. Obviously, Moth could, and would, protect me from any sort of physical danger, but I trust him with my heart. When he landed in my life, that's not something I expected.

"Tonight has been really special," I say, reaching up to put my arms around his neck. "I just—I don't think anyone's ever taken care of me afterward like this."

"Well," he leans down, planting a small kiss on my forehead, "it is a good thing you have me now."

I let myself relax as his claws rake through my hair until it's smooth and slick down my back. He dries me off with the fluffiest towel available before we're both back in the blanket-nest that is my—*our*—bed.

I've tried not to think about what would happen when he went home, not realizing that he's already here. I let my eyes go heavy while he idly plays with my hair.

I love you, I want to say, but the words never reach my mouth.

20.

OUR BODIES THREAD TOGETHER LIKE A knit blanket; by the time morning light hits the windows, it's stuffy, and my arm is falling asleep. But I make no attempt to move. Last night was perfect, and as soon as I move a muscle, I have to admit that it's over. Before last night, I wasn't sure who I was to Moth—a witch in the woods, a weak creature to protect, an insufferable human. If destiny and fate exist, I don't think the two of us in bed together was part of the plan. But here we are, and nothing has ever felt so right.

I brush my fingers through his midnight hair, breathing in the scent of oak and leaves after a storm. "Hi," I murmur.

"Good morning."

His claws trail down the length of my face. With the sun streaming through the windows, we laze in contented silence until Moth gets up. He returns with a glass of water and my pill case. "You require this?"

My heart flutters in my chest. I can't believe he noticed something this small. It's not like I make a big show of taking my medication every morning; it's so ingrained in my routine, most days I don't even think about it.

"Thanks." I sense there's a question on his lips, but he doesn't ask even as I swallow the pill and gulp the water. "I'm fine, by the way." The tension in his shoulders eases as the words leave my mouth. "I have something called Hashimoto's; honestly, it sucked before I learned to manage it." I shrug, not wanting to make it a big thing.

Going gluten-free helped a little for the inflammation. I've always been jealous of people who have thyroid problems and can still tolerate it. I'm not sure how to explain to him that it's just a part of my normal life. "I just need to take a pill every morning, and get bloodwork done a few times a year, but the flares can be the worst."

"What causes these flares?"

"Food, hormonal shifts. For me, stress is a big one."

"So, when you took to your bed for an entire day..."

"That wasn't—I was just like, feeling—"

—like I was sinking into the bed. Like everything around me was numb and spiraling at the same time. Like my bones ached, and my brain was foggy.

"Oh shit, it actually might have been—at least partly. I don't know. down up just a day or two." Stretching my arms up to the sky, I let out a relaxed sigh. Today is anything but *that* feeling. "Honestly, it's hard to tell when I'm burning out when everything feels so … calm. Back in Orlando, there would be weeks I'd be so focused on creating content I swear I could sustain myself on iced coffee. I'm not always great at like … taking care of myself."

Moth gently cups my hand in his hands. "There will be no more of that." He has a way of looking at me like I'm the only person in the world. "Still, I worry I have been the cause of your unease."

Moth's angular face is shaded in guilt, though I'm not sure why. Yeah, there have been a few bumps in the road, but this is the steadiest I've felt in a long time.

"Oh *please*." I pull him in close and plant a kiss on his nose, which he wrinkles as soon as my lips make contact. Cute—so cute. "All this has been a walk in the park compared to Fashion Week with my mom."

"This has been one of the best mornings of my life," I admit, letting my head fall onto his firm chest.

The next hour is spent with our lips and limbs entangled until Moth once again leaves to retrieve tea and a bowl of berries. It's like we're a couple on their honeymoon. We share kisses, feeding each other berries until my body finds its way on top of his. My lips press against his, slick with juice, hungry and wanting. With ease, he hoists me up so that I'm straddling his hips.

"I am never going to get tired of this," I whisper in his ear.

I can feel the curve of his grin against my neck. He rolls so that he's on top of me, and my body crashes into the nest of pillows.

"Good," he says.

I laugh as he dives forward, kissing down the length of my neck. The touch of his bare skin on mine is enough to make me moan. He's so perfectly warm; it's as though I'm curled up in the world's most muscular sweater. My body pulses at the memory of how he made me feel last night.

"Do you want more?" he taunts in a low voice. I nod, placing my hands on top of his to guide them lower. His fingers slip past the hem of my nightgown, letting the fabric bunch at my hips—and oh, oh my god.

If the moans coming from my lips aren't enough, I'm sure he can feel the way my body responds to his touch. The need I feel when he touches me is unbearable, lovesick, and greedy. I pull him closer, melting against each curling movement of his fingers. The warmth of his wings wraps around me as my body turns to unsteady jelly.

I always knew Moth could destroy me with the flick of his fingers. I just didn't think it would be like this.

"Oh my—yes—*oh!*" I try and fail to tell him I'm close; a playful spark in his eyes lets me know he gets the idea. His steady rhythm picks up, building waves of pleasure through me. I hold tight to his shoulders, burrowing my face in his collarbone.

With just a few more movements, he has me breathless, boneless, and completely satisfied. I cuddle up beside him.

"You are—I can't—just like—what?" I don't know what to say to him.

"I—" He pauses, searching my face. "You are happy?"

I pull him into a hug, squeezing his body tight to mine. "Very."

"I enjoyed that." The back of his hand brushes against my upper thigh. "I enjoy you."

"I uh—do you want—or need—"

"There is much time to explore each other." A kiss lands on my cheek that somehow feels more intimate than anything we've done so far. There's playful mischief to his eyes that makes him appear suddenly cat-like.

"But you, my love, require rest." He kisses my hand, and I catch sight of the row of fangs with the slight curve of his smile. *My love, flame, and flower*—everything he calls me makes me feel precious and wanted. I'm not just some conquest or hookup to him; this—whatever it is between us—might be the most real thing I've ever felt. I was worried that it would be the end of something when morning came, but now I see we're just at the beginning

I want to make him feel just as amazing as I do, but that would require moving from this spot, which is so not going to happen.

He slips away to draw us a bath, which makes me feel like I'm in some historical romance novel. The room smells like hot steam and lavender, and there's a plate of berries perched precariously on the rim that Moth knocks over as soon as he eases his giant body into the tub.

He's predictably and comically too large, but that doesn't stop us from trying to cram our bodies together. We're going to need an indoor hot-tub or something if we want to take baths together. He sits on the edge, braiding my damp hair into a crown. Honestly, had I known he had this kind of skill, I would have asked him to start braiding my hair weeks ago. Not only is the touch of his fingers on my scalp hypnotic, but the braid looks legitimately good. I stay in the water till my skin is wrinkled.

Moth leaves me only to sort out the mess from last night. He apologizes for the death of my porcelain poodle collection, but when I tell him it's an excuse to buy more poodles, he grimaces. "You have odd taste." He slips onto his knees to kiss my forehead before I get out of the bath.

"Lucky for you."

"Indeed." He pulls me in for another kiss, and I close my eyes, savoring the way his soft lips feel on my skin. How do I tell him that in just a few short weeks he's become my favorite person?

By the time I get out, Moth has cleared the cabin of all traces of broken glass and splintered picture frames. I slip into an old Gunne Sax dress and flop into the couch next to him. If only every morning could be this good.

"Could I… uh, you know what? Never mind."

"*Tell* me."

"You're going to laugh."

"Has that ever stopped you?"

I narrow my eyes, but he's right. The thing is, I'm not scared of looking silly; I'm afraid he'll say no.

"I want a picture of you." I dip my head so that my hair hangs like a curtain in front of my face. I'm not used to feeling this bashful around him. I had far more intimate requests for him the night before, but the question hangs in the air, circling around us like a leaf in the wind.

"What?" The couch shifts; he's standing now, pacing the room.

The sharpness of his tone is enough to pull me out of my self-made curtain. Moth looks guarded. He moves toward me as if wearing a suit that's too tight on his shoulders. I can't help but notice how his large frame fills the room. With all the shifting around, the top of his wings keeps brushing against the roof. Sometimes, it looks like he's crammed inside a dollhouse.

"It's just—before, whenever I wanted to remember something forever, I'd take a picture of it. Obviously, I'm not going to share them anywhere, but it feels weird that I don't have one of you." I have no desire to share my monster-boyfriend with anyone, especially my unadoring public. A picture is just the closest thing I have to putting this moment in a bottle.

He pulls me up off the couch, and his forehead falls to rest on my own. He nods into me with a shaky breath, and I contain my squeal of glee.

"Together," he agrees.

He watches diligently as I set the stage. I didn't pack any of my equipment except for my camera, so I strategically place the lamps and balance the camera on a stack of books.

I decide to use the loveseat as the focal point, framing us with a few potted plants. It's not the most polished setup, but something about the composition just works. The yellow glow of the lamps gives us an appealing incandescence.

After flicking the camera's settings to the automatic self-timer, I sit down to take a quick test photo. Moth leans over the back of the couch, his wings sprawled wide as his lips press against my forehead, warm and tender. He glances warily up at the blinking camera.

"Just try to ignore it," I tell him. These shots should feel as much like our daily lives as possible. The whole point is to capture a moment in time. So, I bring us two cups of cocoa; we cheer with our mugs and share sweet marshmallow kisses. The best kind of pictures are when you forget the camera is even there. Luckily, I remember before we go too far.

I stand to begin to clear up the mess, and Moth rises to help. I squeeze him tightly around his waist. It's moments like this that our height difference is really apparent. The top of my head just barely reaches where his chest begins.

"Maybe I should put on some heels." I laugh as if I even own a pair that would be tall enough. Moth effortlessly pulls me up by the waist, his lips brushing against my jaw before finding my lips.

"You are not going anywhere." His teeth nip at my earlobe before gently biting down, sending shivers through my entire body.

"Don't you want to see how the pictures turned out?" I tease, letting my hands trail down his abdomen.

"As much as you've piqued my curiosity," Moth whispers, his breath hot on my neck, "there is something more I desire."

I squeal playfully, pushing him away. I expect him to hold me tighter, but he respects the distance I placed between us. His posture, however, resembles a predator poised to attack. I gulp, meeting the heady look in his eyes. I'm tempted to ask him to take me again right here and now. But I'm already a little sore, and like he said earlier, we have time.

He exhales as if resisting me is a chore; it fills me with a powerful feeling I don't know what to do with. It's not that I've never felt desired before, but under Moth's gaze, I feel as though I'm being worshipped—there's no request too silly or strange.

He wants to please me, and I want to let him. But I'm way too curious about how we look together in photographs to think about anything else.

I lead him to the couch, flopping my legs overtop of his, and we cuddle together as I flip through the pictures. The lighting worked out in our favor: there's a warm glow to our skin and the room is bathed in shadow.

"You have talent."

The compliment makes me flush; I steady myself against him, tucking my body close to his.

"You told me you would write stories to go along with your shared photographs." His voice gives me goosebumps. "What would you write as our story, my flame?"

"When words aren't enough, I'll settle for a kiss," I decide, planting my lips against his cheek in a surprise attack. It's just the encouragement he needs to seize me by the waist. In seconds, I'm pinned against the arm of the loveseat as tender kisses work their way down my neck.

"Bite me," I groan, and he obediently sinks his fangs into my flesh in a sharp kiss that makes me rock against him.

"What if you transformed?" My request comes in a voice so quiet I'm not sure it's my own.

"For one of your photographs?" His red eyes flick to the camera with hesitation. Capturing his human form is one thing, but no, I wouldn't ask that of him.

"No..." I reach out, gingerly running my fingers up his chest. "For me, while we..."

"Oh ... *oh*." His mouth clamps shut, and his expression becomes unreadable. "Does this form not ... please you?"

"No! It does! I just, I don't know..."

"You are curious. I suppose I cannot blame you." He gives me a once over, and a slight smirk plays on his lips. "If you could transform, I would also ... wonder."

"It was a silly question; I'm sorry."

"Do not apologize." He lets out a sigh. "I understand you cared for me in that form; you have seen it. I do not understand why you would want to see it again, but I... no—not now."

"Are you worried about hurting me?"

"I am worried you will be frightened." He says the words like it's obvious. I wish Moth would stop forgetting I chose all of him. "For whatever reason, the fates have driven you into my life. I simply cannot seem to do without you, and I will not lose you. Not if I can help it."

"Moth..."

"I recall how you looked at me the first time we met." He pinches the bridge of his nose, sinking into himself.

20.

"You thought I was what? Hunting you? Considering the circumstances, I do not blame you but—"

I wish I could be mad, but I get it; no one wants to be rejected, not even Mothman. It's his body. I'm not going to pressure him into how he uses it. So, I lie close to his warm, mostly human skin, without a single complaint.

"I'm not going anywhere." I snuggle tighter in his arms and feel him exhale.

"You are not allowed."

"Oh, so tough," I say, planting a firm kiss on his lips, pulling his large body on top of mine. "As if I'm not the one holding you captive."

His teasing mouth against mine, the feather-soft brush of his skin, is the sweetest torment. Nothing could ruin this moment.

BEEP BEEP BEEP!

A car horn shouts from outside. What the hell? Even out in the middle of nowhere, my love life is getting interrupted.

"Honey!" *Oh hell no.* I'd know that voice anywhere.

I rush toward the window and catch sight of a navy-blue Mini Cooper with a "Live Laugh Love" bumper sticker on the back. I learned how to drive sitting in that very driver's seat, got car-sick in the back during family road trips, and sang along to top 40 hits with the AUX cord snaking between an ancient iPod and the old cassette player.

In a world of high paced travel, trips, and house upgrades, this car is a reminder of a a simpler time when the world felt smaller. I think Mom has always felt the same sort of nostalgia because no matter how big the paycheck, she's refused to get rid of it.

The bigger question is, what is it doing parked in my driveway?

21.

"YOU HAVE TO LEAVE!" I WHISPER, rushing Moth toward the door—or should it be the window? Could he even fit out the window?

Moth straightens.

"Did you not *just say* I was stuck with you?"

"Not leave forever! Oh my god." I pace back and forth, raking my hair through the loose tendrils of hair that have escaped my braided crown. "It's my mom!"

"And you want me to leave?" The way he says it makes my heart feel like it's been smashed into a million pieces. But even with his wings hidden, I do not want to be explaining why there's a strange, very tall man in my house.

"You do not get along?" He presses as if she isn't about to knock our door clean off its hinges.

"No—well not lately—but it's complicated." And it always has been. The thing is my childhood was great for the most part: matching outfits, matching poses, and tiny pairs of novelty sunglasses. Making content with my mom had always felt like one big game, except for the days it didn't. Mom did her best. I'm thankful for the life we had together, but I wonder when the line blurred between me being her daughter and part of her brand. Over the past few years, our relationship has felt more like a business arrangement, which is probably my fault. But do the two of us get along?

"Yes! No! I—" I sigh. "Look, I already have a lot I need to explain to her. Please just go. You wanted to stretch your wings, right?"

His eyes glint red. I can't tell if he understands or is offended, but Moth gets the message.

"Yes… I would hate to be *one more thing*."

"You know what I mean!"

Why is she here? Why didn't she say she was coming? Mom knows I've always hated surprises. I know she's been worried, but to just show up unannounced? Yes, I'm her kid, but I'm also, you know, a full-grown adult. She should trust me to live my own life.

The curtains billow around the open window. Sure, I asked Moth to leave, but he could have at least said goodbye. With a huff, I head to the bathroom to splash cold water on my face and run a comb through my dyed hair.

I quickly change out of last night's clothes into dark jeans and a cream-colored sweater.

When I pull the door open, Mom looks perfect as always; her blonde hair is in soft waves, and she's dressed in a simple sundress with a pair of oversized sunglasses obscuring her expression.

"Mom?"

"What did you do to yourself?" Her elegant hands reach out to touch my newly dyed tresses.

Mom has always loved my hair. I once got a dramatic pixie cut in middle school, and she cried for a week. We don't look much alike, not really. The honey-blonde color I had was my connection to my brand—and to her. It made people ask if she was my older sister and swoon over what a cute mother-daughter duo we were when we wore matching styles.

My shoulders fall forward. I knew she'd be disappointed in my hair, but I didn't think my appearance would be the first thing she'd comment on. "I needed a change," I reply, brushing the strands back.

"And uprooting your life wasn't enough?" She doesn't yell—no, she never really has been the type. As grateful as I am for that, the heartbreak in her eyes might be worse than anger.

I hate it when she's disappointed in me. But what's worse is that even as a full-grown adult, I feel like I'm going to burst into tears. All I've ever wanted was to make her happy.

"Did you drive here just to berate me about my hair?" I ask, turning my face away.

Her arms wrap around me, catching me in a surprisingly warm hug. I freeze, reeling from the sudden affection.

"Of course not. You're beautiful no matter what." She says it as if she's reading off of a script. I don't know that I believe her, but I cave, giving in to the embrace. I missed her too much to push her away right now.

"Thanks, Mom." I gulp, stepping aside to let her into the house. It's so obvious the minute I turn that I haven't been alone.

Two mugs.

Two plates.

Two lives shared within these walls.

"This would be a great place for a photo shoot," Mom exclaims.

"Mom."

"Oh, come on. I see your camera set up in the living room. If you needed a trip to get reinspired, you should have just said so. Remember that time we went to Bali? We both came home so refreshed. There's nothing like a little room service to get the creative juices flowing again."

I swipe my camera off the pile of books before she can chance to catch a glimpse of my new romantic photoset. "What are you doing out here?" I ask, interrupting her reminiscing.

"When you stopped calling me, I got worried. Then, you wouldn't return my calls, so I—"

My phone.

The memory of Moth crushing it in his hands comes rushing back. We've been so *busy* I'd completely forgotten.

"Ah—I kinda—well, it broke." I shrug as if it hasn't been an extension of my hand as soon as I could hold it. "I haven't gotten out to the store to replace it."

21.

"So, you just … haven't had a phone at all?" Her mouth hangs open "Honey, what if there was an emergency?"

I can't exactly tell her that, up until this moment, I've had a wounded, yet very strong, moth-creature living in my house. I need something—anything—to distract her from asking any more questions.

"Let's get to that photoshoot, huh?" I say, as we step into the bedroom during my "less than grand tour." I eye the sad, neglected ballgown I brought just in case. Of course, you never know when you're going to need a ballgown. "But only if you promise to dress up and don't post any photos."

The worried creases on Mom's forehead disappears. Thank goodness she's easy to distract.

"Deal!"

We rummage through my closet and find the fanciest pieces I packed—which, admittedly, is probably too many. Moth was right when he called me frivolous. I'm lucky that it's a trait that he's attracted to because I'm a fancy-dress-in-the-middle-of-the-woods kind of lady. That's never going to change. We rummage through my closet and at first, it feels like exactly what it is: a distraction. But it's also kind of fun. This was always my favorite part of content creation—putting together fun looks, running around and making up stories, dressing up as different characters, and creating cool self-portraits that filled me with life.

I didn't think I'd ever get that feeling back again, but this has at least been fun. I can't remember the last time we did something so low-key and DIY. With mom's popularity, she has a professional photographer in every state these days, which was honestly kind of amazing. But I still remember when it was just the two of us with a self-timer in our small over-decorated apartment. Even with all the unsaid words and heavy emotions, it's strange how easily we can bounce back into this familiar feeling.

I choose a blue selkie-style chiffon dress while Mom goes for more of a vintage gardener-inspired look. I snap pictures of her pretending to tend to the empty garden beds in the front of the house and sweeping the cabin floors, which honestly needed to be swept anyway.

For my photos, I adorn the braid crown Moth gave me with brambles and lie in the grass.

"I want to look like I'm the queen of the forest," I explain before we jump in. Mom pulled her blonde hair up and put her sunglasses back on. She has her own DSLR around her neck and snaps the pictures thoughtfully as I meld with my surroundings.

It's different than how it felt when I set up the camera to take pictures with him; that was cozy and intimate. When Mom looks through the camera, she sees the exact story I'm trying to tell, and the two of us bounce back and forth trying to bring it to life.

As far as distractions go, it's a good one. We take turns snapping photos until the sun is low in the sky. Then, I look up toward the roof and see the shadow of wings.

"Why don't you head in and take a shower before dinner?" I suggest, trying to keep my eyes from darting toward Moth's silhouette on the roof. I would worry I look strange to him, but he's seen my closet. Still, it feels oddly vulnerable.

21.

It's not hard to convince Mom to go inside and get first dibs on the hot water. I, however, linger outside, pretending like I haven't noticed the sizeable, winged man perched on my roof. "I'll uh, be in in a minute."

I stand on the porch until the sun's last glow has faded, and Moth's red eyes beckon me toward the edge of the woods. I'm not sure when he swooped down from the roof, but I'm taken by the sight of him.

A devil has never looked so angelic, I'd caption his portrait

"Come here." I'm swallowed by the darkness in his voice.

As if hypnotized, I walk forward until the glow of his eyes makes me squint.

His breath brushes across my skin. "I'd like to kiss the queen of the forest."

I can't believe he heard that. But I don't have time to be embarrassed. Moth bends his tall body to meet my lips. He's tender at first, meeting me with gentle kisses until our bodies are pressed together, and my hands start to wander when he lets out a groan.

"I should go," I whisper, enjoying the thrill of teasing him again.

"Tonight," he says, pulling me back. "Meet me outside your window."

My body shudders at the memory of his touch. Last night was *wow*, and it's just the beginning.

"There is something I wish for you to see."

"You don't say?" I stand on my tiptoes, but still, my lips barely graze his jaw. I pluck a flower from my crown and stick it behind his ear. "Tonight." I boop his nose before practically skipping into the house.

I'd hoped Mom might be staying at a hotel. Instead, I literally had to stay up, waiting for her to fall asleep before sneaking out to meet my boyfriend.

I never had a rebellious phase as a teenager. I guess I'm making up for it now. In her mind, I'm some delinquent runaway; playing the part is the least I can do. A giddy feeling rushes through me as Moth leads me to a thicket of trees with a hollow at the center, a cloth strung up like a makeshift door.

He pushes it aside and allows me to enter first.

The "room" is littered with a discarded basket, novels soaked from the rain, a hair ribbon faded from sunlight, shining bottle caps, and a few shirts that look centuries old. There's a piece of parchment with words and symbols I don't recognize. I trace the letters with my index finger before my eyes drift to an old-fashioned silk shirt. It looks like something from a costume shop, only the fabric feels as soft as butter and seems to have an iridescent shine. I bet it would photograph like starlight. My lips raise in a smile when I catch sight of my Jane Austen novel in the corner. Judging by the leaf stuck between the pages, he's been reading it in his free time.

This place seems surprisingly sentimental for someone who claims they don't care about their past.

Something gleams from within the hollow of the tree. A crown hangs on a piece of bark that protrudes like a hook. I pick up a circlet—it's stunning and appears woven from golden leaves and uncut amber gemstones. God, I would have killed to use something like this for a photoshoot.

But what is Moth doing with it?

As I hold the crown in my hands, a knot forms in my chest. Am I not the first self-made model who wandered around these woods?

I don't ask before placing it on my head. "How's that for the queen of the forest?" I stick out my tongue, turning back to him.

Moth does not laugh. Instead, his fingers trail from my waist to my jaw, sending shivers with each touch. "It was as if it was waiting for your possession."

"I have a hard time believing you just found something this gorgeous in the woods."

"Why?" Moth tilts his head. "I found you, did I not?" His toothy, crooked grin is endearing, even with the row of fangs, as sharp as knives.

Moth seems to have a fondness for lost things. Maybe that's why he brought me here.

"This is where you went when you disappeared?"

"Yes."

"I imagined you'd have, like, a bed made of moss and leaves or something."

"I am sorry to disappoint."

"I do not think you could."

We regard each other for a long moment with no sound except for the wind whispering through the trees. A gust pushes me forward until my body tumbles into Moth's. I guess even the woods themselves wants us to kiss. Luckily, I agree.

"So, you've brought me to your collection of lost things." I give him a half-smile, lowering my lashes and raising them in a way I hope looks playful and not like a weird extra-long blink. "I don't think there's a shelf big enough for me..."

His eyes are wide and glassy; his stare is so intense that, if I don't look away, I think I might shatter. My pulse quickens as he looks into the very depths of my soul.

"Moth..." I breathe as his hands rest upon the small of my back.

"You misunderstand," he whispers. "I am the one who has been found."

This whole time...

He's felt just as lost as I have.

My lips are on his before I can stop myself.

Heat burns through me. It takes every ounce of control not to melt onto the ground of this clearing we're standing in. I close the distance between us, my head resting on his chest. "If you keep saying stuff like that—"

His mouth meets mine in a firm kiss before I can finish the sentence. His tongue pours into my mouth while his claws stroke my back; each sensation is more delicious then the next. My body pulses with waves of pleasure until my limbs are frozen solid.

"What will you do?" He lifts me, pressing me back against the rough bark of a tree. My legs wrap around his torso, the cold air prickling my newly exposed skin. Moth clutches my body to his with just one arm curled around my waist. His other skillfully works its way up the soft curves of my body.

"Damn," I whisper. The things he can do with just a kiss.

It's good. Too good.

At my groan, he begins to untangle himself from me. "Do you want me to stop?" His voice and grip soften. I shake my head, pulling him closer.

"No, please." I gasp. "I mean, unless you don't want to—mmm."

His lips silence any over-thinking I could propel myself into. Wanting Moth is easy. But in the hollow of this tree, with this gorgeous otherworldly man looking down at me, I'm his spark, a fire intent on making him ache. The agony in his eyes makes me realize just how much he's been burning for me

I can't understand what he sees in me.

"What I want..." He smirks. His lips find my collarbone, and his fangs nibble at my skin, teasing low moans from me with each taste of my flesh. His clawed fingers sink into my hair, scratching the base of my scalp in a way that makes my whole head tingle.

"Anything," I whisper in his ear. In response, his whole body shudders. "If you wanted to eat me alive, I think I'd let you."

"Would you?" His voice is like silk across my skin; he presses kisses lower and lower, following the ache of my body until the monster of the woods is on his knees in front of me.

I gulp, nodding.

His large hands slide up the length of my thighs. With the drag of a single claw—*snick*!—my high-waisted panties are laid to waste. His fingertips circle over flesh until they're replaced with his mouth. He alternates kissing and touching until his tongue works its magic. It's been so long since I've felt anything like this. *No*, I've *never* felt anything quite like this before. His fangs carefully graze my sensitive skin, and I moan at the new sensation.

"Absolute perfection." He punctuates each word with a kiss, regarding me as though I'm a sculpture in an art gallery. Moth's hands grip my hips and with long, broad strokes, his tongue teases and circles until I think I might break. It curls up again and again until heat spreads through my body, starting low and traveling upward until my face feels like it's on fire. My fingers claw into his shoulders as I bend and buckle with each pressing motion.

"*I*—"

He moans praises and encouragement, melting me with each deep kiss. I grip the hair on the nape of his neck so hard I'm worried I'll tear it out.

"That's it." His deep, soothing voice echoes through my body and pulls me over the edge. The simple words ring through me as I shudder, crashing into his arms. His dark wings drape around me like a second skin as my legs buckle.

"I have you," he whispers, and he does. I am entirely and devastatingly his. No more mental games with myself, no more resisting; home is to be safe in his arms, and isn't that what I came out here to find?

After spending so many years virtually surrounded, yet completely alone, maybe I'm ready to lean on someone. Especially if that someone is him.

I pounce, and we topple onto the bed of leaves below us. He's reduced my bones to a pile of jelly, but I push up until my thick thighs straddle his waist. Moth's eyebrow quirks, an amused smile playing upon his lips.

21.

"*My, my,* it seems I still have work to do." He tilts his head in an owlish way that doesn't quite suit his human form.

With his hardness pressing between my thighs, his desire is clear.

"Work, huh?" I lean down, planting a kiss at the tip of his nose. "Is there a spreadsheet you need to get to or—"

A growl comes from his chest—it's playful in tone but sends my body back into a shivering needy state. The things this man can do with his voice alone.

Tenderly, he trails a claw up the length of my body. Want and admiration sparks in his crimson eyes; even in his human form, they seem to glow in the darkness.

"*Very good.*" The ring of his praise in my ear has me rocking my hips on top of him until I ache for more. "I want you senseless with pleasure."

"You're so good at this—*how* are you so good at this?"

"I have had dalliances."

Of course, he's been with other people. Nothing about the way our bodies meet is amateur or clumsy. Uncertainty attempts to take root in my chest; I'm not usually a jealous person, but the thought of him with anyone else makes me feel crestfallen—despite being the one right here in his arms.

"That's not all I am to you, is it?" Sensing my new hesitation, Moth has stopped moving under me. "A *dalliance in the dark* or whatever?"

"How could you be?" With ease, he sits up, pulling me into his lap. I'm soothed by the richness of his voice, and his claws raking through my hair. "When you illuminate these woods so beautifully?"

"I've been with other people too." I don't know why I say it. He's over here spouting poetry and I—God—maybe I want to make him jealous too. Once I start, the words keep coming. "Women, men, people who don't fit into that narrow binary…" I've always been pretty open about my sexuality. Most of the people I meet know me from the internet. I haven't had to *come out* to anyone since high school. I've mostly been lucky, but not everyone responds well. Who knew my nervous ramble could end up being this vulnerable?

"As have I." He nods, as if we're talking about something as causal as the weather, but the nod he gives me is patient and understanding. He quirks an eyebrow. "Are you attempting to make me jealous, my flame?"

"No—yes—I don't think so. Now that you mention it, the last time you were jealous was pretty fun and I wouldn't mind if we—"

My words are cut short by his lips. It feels playful, and though I catch a glint of that possessive nature he had the other night, his gaze is sweet and filled with something neither of us have expressed out loud.

Love.

"I see you, Heather."

Relief floods through me as I place a small kiss on his pointed nose. I want to hold tight to the softness of this moment. The next kiss is tender and agonizingly slow in a way that makes the muscles in my back build with tension. "I want you on top of me," I whisper in his ear.

He shivers before grabbing hold of my waist and rolling so that his body cages mine. Little twigs hang like confetti in his dark curls.

21.

"So beautiful." His antennae bobble when he speaks the words. When I reach up to stroke the stiff feather-like appendages, I'm happy he doesn't snatch my hand away. No, this time he leans into my touch and his long eyelashes flutter closed.

"Don't make me beg again," I whisper. He quakes at the words—it's nice to know my words can cause a reaction in him too. A sheen of sweat glistens across his firm chest. Hooking my legs around his waist, I pull him in as deep as he can go and groan into his shoulder at the way we fit together. Last night was hard and fast—and everything I had fantasized about—but the admiration in his eyes tonight takes my breath away. Each touch of his fingertips is gentle and devoted to bringing my body unbridled pleasure. He grits his teeth, the row of fangs dazzlingly white under the pale moon. When our gazes meet again, his gemstone eyes are half-lidded in ecstasy.

"Fuck, you're pretty," I remark. He barks out a laugh, his grin wide and unguarded. I meet him with each thrust until he writhes into a shuddering mess on top of me.

There's something about seeing such a strong person unravel—something that makes me feel powerful and giddy. With a few skillful movements, I'm pulled into euphoria by the tips of his fingertips. Soon, we're both out of breath with lazy smiles on our faces.

In the middle of these woods, there is just us—just this moment.

His chest presses against mine. "Now," Moth nuzzles into my shoulder with the causal intimacy of a couple that's been together for years—not weeks "*what* is a spreadsheet?"

The night air once filled with moans of pleasure now sings with my laughter. Moth covers me in kisses as he wraps me in his warm arms.

Yes, I think I'm definitely going to keep him.

22.

IT DIDN'T TAKE LONG TO FIND MY MOM VLOGging from my kitchen. But here she is, showing her followers my home—a place I didn't invite them into.

"What are you doing?" I snatch her phone out of her hand.

"I'm just posting a tiny update; I'm not tagging you or your location; it's no big deal." She laughs.

"Does 'we're taking these just for fun?' ring a bell?" Ugh, I should have known better before letting her get behind a camera.

"Honey, you're overreacting."

"Oh my god. You've already posted, haven't you?"

"People have missed seeing us together." Her smile is so bright and steady; it's the kind of face that makes your anger just melt away. But not today.

I look away. "Because god forbid you spend just one normal weekend with me," I say. "It's bad enough you came out here to check up on me."

"Who wants to be *normal*?" She loops her arm in mine, pulling me toward a fresh pot of coffee she must have brewed.

"Me!" I shake my arm away from hers. "Why do you think I'm out here?!"

"Honey, I said normal—not Amish." She wrinkles her nose, swiping her thumb across her phone screen. She laughs as she types. Knowing mom, she's probably live-posting this conversation. "Honestly, I don't understand this obsession with unplugging."

"Maybe because my entire life has been broadcasted by you? Maybe I don't want my morning to be monetized?" I pick up the small-batch coffee she brewed—the one I caught her taking a selfie with moments ago. "Let me guess: this week's sponsor? Can't you just exist with me for five minutes?"

"Oh..." She stumbles back as if I delivered a physical blow. "No, no, Honey—*Heather*—I always thought of all of it as a big scrapbook. You know that."

"Scrapbooks don't normally pay the bills."

"That's not fair. You know what I mean." She runs her hands through her perfect blonde hair, and for a moment, I wish mine was still that same shade. Even out here in the wilderness, she's effortless. The woman is a walking #nofilter. Still, it doesn't make up for the fact that she isn't listening.

"Did you ever think that maybe sharing the details about potty training your toddler might cross a boundary?" I jam my hands in my pockets, refusing to look at her anymore. "Like, did you know people have googled me after our dates and have found all of this embarrassing shit?"

"Hey!" She raises an eyebrow. "Just because you're mad doesn't mean you get to use that language with me."

"We're both adults, Mom. If me swearing is what you're going to focus on in this conversation, we have bigger issues."

She's silent for a long moment.

"I figured no one cared about that stuff. Back when I was writing it, I was a single mom. I didn't have friends or a community, and my blog was everything. My readers always made me feel like I had support, like I wasn't in it alone." She reaches out, her hand grazing my arm. "And don't get me wrong: you were, and still are, the best decision I've ever made. But it was lonely those first couple of years."

"I know, Mom." It's not the first time she's talked about this. I know how hard it was for her, how much her ever-growing internet family has meant to her. But it doesn't change the facts. "It's just… my whole life is out there for people to watch. You vlogged my birth!"

"Oh, I did not. Vlogging wasn't even a thing back then, and the full video is behind a paywall! The public only got the highlights."

"*Mom*!" I don't know how she doesn't hear herself. I understand that these are all big moments for her, but it's my life too, and I never got a choice. Everything from my first breakout to my last breakup is written about from a mother's point of view. Whenever I made an offhand comment or joke about my lack of privacy, she was always quick to remind me that this was her job. Her *art*.

But I've never really told her how I felt.

"It's a lot of pressure being the daughter of the great @MarshaMallowLatte, you know?" I comb my fingers through my brown hair. "I bet they're already criticizing this," I add, pulling at the newly dyed strands.

"No," she says in a tone reserved for absolute lies. I give her a pointed look. "Okay, okay, maybe a little. But I taught you better than to care, right?"

"Yeah, no, right. Of course." I sigh. Of course, she did. Ignore the trolls. Don't read the comments. But also, I've been trained since birth to perform in front of the camera. A funny comment would get her views, make her smile, and turn a bad day into a good one. It hasn't always been bad, but I'm a child star in the sitcom of her life.

And I'm just *so tired*.

"I understand burnout, taking that time to find your spark again, but you'll bounce back and—what? Why are you giving me that look?"

"I don't want to bounce back," I tell her firmly. "I don't want to share anymore. This place, this life I'm creating? It's just for me, okay? And yeah, you can come to visit, you can be a part of it, but not if you're going to act like a tourist. You don't get to snap like a million pictures or tell your online friends all the details of my life."

I turn away from her, letting out a heavy breath. "Do you know how it feels for someone to come up to you on the street and know everything about you? Your favorite food from when you were a kid? The time you had a tantrum at Disneyworld? They pull up embarrassing photos and tell me they can't believe I've gotten so big. People know things about me that I never even had the choice to share!"

"But you're my daughter—and the things I share—I always—we always..." She's scrambling. It looks like I've hit the factory reset button.

"I want control over my story for once in my life, and I need you to be okay with that. Especially if you want to be a part of it."

"So, we're just supposed to ... be out here together and not talk about it?"

"Yeah."

"No pictures? No stories? No videos?"

"Or you can leave." I'm literally shaking as I say the words. I've never, ever stood up to her like this. Mostly because I've been in denial for so much of our lives together.

"Okay." My heart catches in my throat as she heads toward the door. I knew she'd never understand.

"Okay," I echo.

"Put on your shoes. We're going for coffee."

And despite having a full pot of coffee on the counter, I don't argue.

Mom always wants to have serious conversations over lattes. I would say it's some kind of character flaw, but it's honestly the best. Even when I was a kid, we'd sit in fancy cafes with a trendy latte for her and an overflowing hot cocoa for me. It made talking about fights, bad grades, and bad dates more soothing.

This time, however, it took us a while to get to the overcrowded Starbucks. First, she insisted on taking me to the closest chain store. There, she loaded me up with enough canned goods, batteries, and emergency supplies to last through an apocalypse and of course a new phone which I begrudgingly accepted. Part of me thought she was just stalling, and we'd never land at a coffee shop for our talk. But here we are seated across from each other, and between us are a million words unsaid and two oat milk lattes.

Whatever it is she wants to say in response to my unhinged monologue can't be good, but there's something nice about just letting her take care of me. It's been forever since we've had a day that's unplugged like this. Most times, I was even worse about it than her. Our Mother-Daughter days were filled with asking for advice on business emails, livestreaming while we got ready, or making content together, which wasn't always bad.

"I haven't felt this worried since you went off to college," she begins, breaking the silence.

"You're the one who stopped answering my calls. . . ."

"I know, I know. I'm sorry." She fiddles with a strand of loose hair before tucking it back into its bun. Even now, she's flawless. "I miss you posting."

"*Mom,*" I groan. I am not ready for another lecture on my brand or whatever.

"Whenever I was curious about what you were up to, I could just look and see your face or read a little play-by-play about your day."

"I didn't even know you paid attention," I admit. She hardly ever left comments on my stuff.

"Of course, I do." She slides into the seat next to me and pulls me close like she's done my whole life. "I know I've sometimes done a crappy job showing it, but you're my whole world, Heather. I hope you know that. I love you."

"I love you too, Mom."

"And I may not understand this whole … *thing* you're doing, but I will try to be supportive." She offers me a half-smile. "For what it's worth, I will delete anything you ask me to. The damage might already be done, but you're right: it is your story. I'm sorry it took you moving all the way out here for me to see that."

"That means more than you know."

"It's the least I can do." Her eyes seem unfocused and distant. I can tell I've given her a lot to think about. "To fresh starts?" She raises her latte in the air to meet mine.

"To fresh starts."

We decide to stop somewhere for dinner.

Mom insists on the fanciest restaurant nearby; neither of us expected it to be a hunting lodge. After Rosie and Clara waved us in from the bar, we somehow ended up stuck between the busts of a deer and a buffalo which is only mildly unsettling.

"It's good to see you." Rosie has a hard time looking me in the eye at first. Since the argument at The

General Store, I've had time to cool off, but I wonder if she feels guilty for not speaking up.

"It's good to see you too." I offer an easy smile, hoping it gets the message there's no hard feelings between us across. Rosie's been here a lot longer than I have; the way she stayed silent while Chris and his friends mocked me wasn't cool. Maybe she felt as powerless as I did, but that's a conversation for another time.

Mom hits it off with them right away, which isn't a surprise. She's never had a hard time getting along with my friends. They tease me relentlessly about the floral wreath while making plans to have a gardening day as we all order and eat our meals together.

Moth and I had planned to fix up the garden beds together. I smirk at the thought of him wearing one of my giant sunhats, planting seeds. But I like Rosie and Clara, and Moth can either don his disguise or get out of the house for the day. Just because I'm dating a cryptid doesn't mean I can't have a social life. Dinner is over too soon, and before I know it, we're saying goodbye to Ohio's cutest couple.

"Okay, we'll plan for some time tomorrow to do the garden?" Clara asks, slinging her leather jacket over Rosie's shoulders. "I've been testing a gluten free cornbread recipe with you in mind."

"You are both way too good to me," I say, extending my arms to squeeze the pair in a hug. "Yes, and yes, I'll throw together chili or something."

After they leave, Mom and I linger in the bar. We ultimately decide we're not ready for the night to end. After my bonfire, I'm not drinking anything stronger than a Shirley Temple. Mom, wanting to be supportive and still social, decides to get us a round of virgin margaritas, which honestly just taste like sugar and lime juice.

The door of the lodge swings open, and before I can make sense of what's going on, Chris gathers me in his arms and spins me around like a hero who has returned from war. I catch my mom's raised eyebrows before she hides a chuckle behind a sip of her cheap drink. It's hard to give her a "it's not what you think" look when I'm being spun around the lodge like it's a grand ballroom.

By the time he sets me back on my feet, my vision is blurry and stretched out as though I'm looking through a fish-eye lens. Chris looks like a man who's swallowed the sun. The glow radiates across his skin and makes his eyes gleam. "I did it! I did it, and you're not going to believe the size of this thing. Everyone … *everyone* told me I was crazy. But you—you got to see it, Heather, you—"

"Okay, slow down; what are you—"

"A round for everyone!" he exclaims, slinging an arm around my shoulders. His camouflage jacket smells like sweat and dirt. It reminds me of hugging my soccer player ex after she won her first match.

"Someone must have done well in the hunt today." The bartender cracks a smile along with a beer.

It's Saturday. The hunt was today. My blood runs cold. I take a deep breath to steady myself. Moth promised he'd be safe. Heck, Mom and I have been gone for so long that he's probably in his usual spot on the loveseat, reading a book. Chris caught some big deer or something and is just acting macho. That's got to be it. Moth is safe and at home. Still, the chatter in the bar makes me feel queasy:

"You're never going to believe the size of this thing!"

"If I hadn't seen it with my own eyes, I never would have believed it. "

"Its wings were 15 feet wide."

"20!"

"And Chris was ruthless. The thing could barely fly, and he just *BOOM.*" One of the guy's motions as if he's shooting a gun. I'm going to be sick.

Moth is at home.

He's safe.

He *promised.*

And even in his state, there's no way these guys could take him down. The way these guys are talking about shooting down some helpless bird is almost sad; it's all a part of their cruel game, which Chris was delighted to win.

Ugh. This is what we get for going to a *lodge* for dinner. Mom couldn't just deal with my cooking for one more night? I slink back to her. She seems amused by the boisterous hunters surrounding Chris. He recounts his "heroic tale" with his beer glass in hand; the foam sloshes as he acts out his every move.

"So, we get to this clearing, right? The trees all sort of stop, and there are all these fucking flowers—and there it is crouching at the center."

"That's on my property," I gasp.

Their eyes shift toward me.

"And thank you again for giving me permission to hunt on your land," Chris says gravely. I'm getting the feeling I could get him into so much trouble right now.

22.

He grasps my shoulder in a gesture that I think is supposed to be reassuring. "We got it before it got you. Tonight, you can sleep easier," he whispers, his voice soft and sweet.

I am frozen, numb to the feeling of his hand caressing my cheek. My stomach flips, and the mounding words spoken across the bar crackle like a radio with a bad signal:

"It's a—"

"The most terrifying bird you've ever seen—"

"—rows and rows of sharp teeth!"

"This thing was a was a—"

"BLAM!"

"—monster."

My boyfriend.

23.

WITH ALL THE CHAOS, IT WASN'T HARD to slip away from the crowd. As if my body is on autopilot, I find a backdoor near the restroom of the lodge and search the parking lot for Chris's truck. That's where I find Moth's body, and he's completely unrecognizable. At first, I think he's wrapped in a tarp of something. A strange cocoon protrudes from parts of his skin like a weird slimy sleeping bag.

The rope used to tie him up is tricky, but no worse than a tangled necklace at the bottom of a purse. *Please don't be dead. Please don't be dead.*

The way they have him tied up has left angry bruises against his exposed skin.

23.

I touch his neck; the strange slime hasn't climbed this far up to his body. His red owl eyes barely open. He looks even worse than the night I found him.

Suddenly, a large hand bursts from the cocoon, grabbing my collar. He pulls me toward him, and I expect his hard beak to meet my lips, fangs and all. I would welcome any affection in this moment.

The kiss does not come.

Moth emits an ear-splitting screech I pray isn't audible from the bar. In a single movement, he tears into the front of my shirt, lifting me up off the ground until my feet dangle in midair. It happens so fast that the wind is knocked from my lungs. It would all be so damn hot in the right context.

But he's not here with me right now.

Moth is miles away, picking flowers in the woods with a gun pointed at his chest—and he thinks I'm the one squeezing the trigger. I gulp. With just a flick of his wrist, he could send my body flying down the street.

"It's me—fuckfuckfuck—uh, shit. *Pineapple!*" This isn't how I originally planned to use our safe word, but I scream it out, kicking him square in the chest.

He blinks, his bug-eyes focusing on me. Still, the mask-like features remain and don't soften back into human flesh.

"Heather…" My creature's voice cracks, but it's *him*. His grip finally relaxes. Moth cradles my body against his chest, and I gasp, taking greedy gulps of fresh air. In this form, his body is firm but soft with feathers that wrap me in their comfort. The scent of oak brings me back into my skin. "I did not mean—"

"It's okay, it's okay—I'm okay." With shaking hands, he smooths my hair away from my face, looking me over as if I'm the one who's hurt.

"How?"

"You said you wouldn't be around to save me all the time, right? I didn't make the same promise." It would all sound so much cooler if I could manage to catch my breath. "You're alive, you're okay, we're okay." My anxious words come a mile a minute. "Can you fly? If those assholes hurt your wings, I can cram you in my car again. Rosie and Clara can probably drive Mom home. Yeah, and that will give me enough time to make sure you have some sort of disguise—"

His wings open, shadowing our bodies in darkness; it's impossible to read his expression.

"Okay, so you can fly. Good. Get back to the cabin and—" I make a sad attempt to pull Moth's massive body out of the truck. "I'm sorry. I know this is like so stupidly fucked up, but we need to get you out of here."

This whole thing is sick—and probably illegal, right? Like, I understand Chris thinks he just shot a monster, but half of his hunting buddies described Moth as a "giant bird." I'm sure there's an Audubon Society of Rare Birds that would be so pissed right now.

Moth doesn't budge, his eyes made of pure fire.

"I'm not the one you should be concerned with." His claws splay out one by one, as his attention turns to the hunting lodge.

Wait, no! I pull at his chest. "You can't go after them. It's not right."

I gulp, taking in the sight of him in the moonlight. There's not so much as a stray bullet hole on his skin, and with every agonizingly slow second that passes, the bruises fade. Has he always been able to heal like this? I touch the once wounded wing and think of the time I spent nursing him back to health at home. Our time together had been slow. Those early memories are peppered with fevers and agony; if he so much as flexed his wings, he'd shudder in pain. How is he able to recover from this so fast?

"You can heal?"

"Why should you worry for me?" He exhales, running his fingers through the tuft of feathers on his head. In this form, he blends with the darkness, illuminating the two of us in the red light of his narrowed eyes.

Why should I be worried about him? After everything we've been to each other these last few days, how can he ask a question like that?

"Um, hello, I am obviously in love with you!" I shout, crossing my arms. Blood drains from my face when I realize what I've said. Those unspoken words should have been special, not something I blurted out in a panic, but that doesn't make them any less real.

The distance between our bodies closes. His eyes widen, and his mouth hangs open.

"I could have hurt you." He traces the holes in my shirt. Whatever point he's trying to make is swallowed by my own desire; each touch of his claws against my skin is torture.

"You snapped out of it as soon as you knew it was me—as soon as you realized it was too much." I stroke the flesh of his bone-white cheek. It doesn't matter that he's still in his monster form. He's still the man I love—even if my attempts to wake him reminded me of dealing with a feral cat.

He groans, pressing his forehead against mine. Tonight is the closest he's ever let himself come to me while in this form. I savor it, my arms tight around his waist. Our breath entangles.

"Come on, why would you have revenge when you could have me?" I tease, pulling him closer. We're taking too long—we're too exposed—but I don't want to leave his arms.

"They came into our home," he hisses. "And you would have me do nothing? I am sorry, my flame."

"No, you're not." I bite my lip to keep from crying. "If you don't love me, just say it."

His jaw hangs open. For a moment, I think he's angry—but no, it's something else, something I can't quite figure out. The moon has shifted, and the shadows across his face give me no inkling.

"If I do not love you?" he scoffs. The hinge of his jaw tightens as he grits his teeth. As if I was silly to assume he might actually feel something real for me, and of course it was. For all the heat and midnight promises, I'm just a foolish human, after all.

I deserve more than that.

"When I am through with these men, no one will dare enter our woods. They have forgotten how to be afraid."

Why is he still talking about the hunters? I don't care about any of that. Shoving him away, I cross my arms protectively in front of my body.

"Oh, so this is for us somehow? And wow—*wow*, Moth, way to avoid the question." I blink tears away from my eyes. "Look, if you're going to get your revenge or whatever, just do it—and don't come back."

Don't come back unless you can say you love me back. That's what I want to say, but the sting of rejection is still too fresh.

His eyes linger on the place where he clawed through my shirt. "Heather—"

Not *"my flame," "my flower," "my love."* The knife in my heart twists deeper. He really doesn't care, does he?

"Oh my gosh, just go already!"

Moth should know me well enough to understand that I don't mean it. I want him to hold me tight, gently brush the hair from my forehead, and assure me nothing like this will ever happen again—but he can't make that promise. Before I can pull him back, he's gone.

The man who is so terrified of breaking me just left me in a million pieces. He chose revenge over my arms. For his sake, I hope it's sweeter than my lips.

In a daze, I walk back into the lodge. The life I created with Moth has gone up in smoke. As I replay the argument over and over, I realize it might have been my fault.

"You feeling okay?" Mom looks up from her phone with a frown. "You were in the bathroom for a long time."

"Yeah, no. I—I think we should go home." I catch Chris eyeing me from the bar. He smiles, raising his drink in the air. God, I think I might be sick.

"Well, I already paid our bill. I got a little worried." She smiles at me. "Moms always know when something is wrong—even the horribly pre-occupied ones."

She gives me an apologetic look as she scoops my keys off the table. Just as I start to crumble, she wraps her arm around me. "I'll drive, okay?"

Mom holds me steady while we walk out to the car. Who would have thought she'd be the anchor I needed in this moment?

"Mom?"

"Yeah, Honey?"

"I'm really glad you're here."

I spend the car ride crying about Moth.

Mom thinks he's a guy I'm talking to online.

And *not* a cryptid I met in the woods.

And that his name is Alden.

And that he's decided to *"talk to other people."*

Dancing around the truth is exhausting, to say the least. There isn't an ounce of truth in anything I've said, except for the feelings behind them.

"You came out here to connect with yourself, right?" she asks once we're safely back home at the cabin. "Does this guy really fit into all of that?"

I guess not.

I look around at the space. There are cabinets to paint, walls to decorate, and that's just on the inside. "I am really excited about the garden," I admit.

"Good thing that's our plan for tomorrow then, right?" She pulls me close in a side hug and gives me a kiss on the cheek that catches me by surprise.

I don't think she's done that since I was a little kid.

23.

Spending the rest of the evening in bed with a tension headache wasn't how I hoped to end the night. I try, in vain, to find a comfortable position but am keenly aware of the muscle spasms that radiate through my back.

If Moth were here, I'm sure I'd be able to persuade him to use those big, clawed hands of his to rub out each of the offending knots. But he's gone.

And this time, I don't think he's coming back.

Mom gives me an aspirin and some peppermint oil she keeps in her purse—a remnant of her stint in a healthy living pyramid scheme. It makes my skin tingle and smells like Christmas, so I can't complain.

When her ancient Mini Cooper pulled up to the cabin a few days ago, I couldn't wait for her to turn around and leave. Now, I'm just glad she's here a little longer.

It doesn't change the fact that when the lights are out and the cabin is quiet, I stare at the ceiling, wishing the town's most feared monster was next to me in bed.

Someone tore through the hunting lodge after we left last night. Chris sent me photos of the wreckage: missing taxidermy, dismantled furniture, shattered glassware, and broken windows. Chris swears it was the monster, and the thing is—he's right.

There are fresh claw marks around his neck to prove it. Something made Moth decide to keep him alive.

On the online community hub, there were several complaints about a "winged shadow" swooping around the area. Half of the commenters think that maybe the brownies on the dessert menu were a little extra special. It's surprisingly easy to explain away collective trauma. But the other half have their guns and pitchforks ready.

They're still not sure if it was a monster or a man, but they want justice. Chris is all too happy to lead the hunt.

I'm glad I didn't have to see Moth like that. Was the revenge called for? Yeah, sure, but is the blood under his claws worth sleeping alone?

It isn't lost on me how connected Moth is with nature. When we walked together in the forest, squirrels and birds flitted around him like he was a damn Disney princess. He was the only trophy that walked away from the hunting competition alive. Maybe I should have been more understanding.

At the end of the day, I'm more upset that he didn't come home than about his rampage. Sure, I told him not to, but is a little groveling and begging for forgiveness too much to ask for? I really thought we had something special.

Of course, the ordeal at the lodge is the topic of choice when Rosie and Clara come over to help in the garden.

"I think one of Chris's buddies was messing with him," Rosie theorizes, slipping off a floral gardening glove to wipe the sweat off her brow. "It wouldn't be the first time they've gotten carried away."

"Why are they so obsessed with him?" I ask. "With the monster, I mean."

"When we were teenagers, the monster apparently lunged at Chris during at a party." She rolls her eyes. "I still think it's all B.S.—just a bunch of drunk teenagers getting carried away. I'm going to have to have a serious talk with him about all the rules he broke by going after that thing."

"You know what I think," Clara says, with a hand on her hip. "They poked a bear, and now they're dealing with the consequences. Those guys would taunt ghosts with a Ouija board and act surprised if a demon decided to answer."

"Oh, I went to their little parties—believe me, they did." Rosie dips her head, letting her red hair fall like wisps in front of her face. "Chris has always been there for me though. Back in high school, it was me and the band geeks, and Chris and his Cryptid Club. Gosh, those guys were honestly the nicest. They'd talk for hours about Bigfoot and the Loch Ness monster and, somehow, still got invited to all of the cool parties." Rosie scrunches her nose with a grimace. "It's different now that they moved away. He runs with the worst crowd. It doesn't excuse the way he treated you, though."

"Oh, it's no big dea—"

"No—*seriously*. I'm so sorry for not sticking up for you back at the shop; I'm worried that if I don't toe the line, everyone is going to shut me out."

"I was worried it might be something like that." I give her a small smile that I hope looks reassuring. "No big, okay? Those guys seemed … intense."

"They're just a bunch of loud gym-bros," Clara adds. "They're annoying, but mostly harmless. It was worse when we first got together—not everyone is accepting, but they tend to be a little quieter about it now." She shakes her head with obvious disapproval.

"What made them stop?"

"They realized bigots don't get banana bread," she jokes with a half-smile. Despite her jovial tone, I can see the hurt behind her eyes. I can't imagine what it would have been like to come out in a small town like this. I can't say everyone in my life has been accepting, but I grew up in a pretty liberal bubble. I was twelve when I went on a date with my first girlfriend, Alice. I think she's jet setting in Europe now, running a travel blog with her Parisian fiancé. Their posts are all glamour, filled with close-ups of room service and low-contrast balcony views. Do I know that from getting drunk and scrolling through all my exes' feeds before moving away?

No. I was completely sober.

I don't need booze to make self-destructive choices. Look at me. My type is unavailable cottagecore lesbians and tall, brooding forest monsters.

"Have you ever thought about moving away?" Mom chimes in. "I heard that's great for solving problems."

She's been quieter than usual today. I should have known it was a matter of time before she jumped in with some classic passive-aggressive parenting.

"This is home," Rosie responds, her hand resting on Clara's leg. Her no-nonsense expression doesn't leave much room for argument.

"Speaking of home, next time I visit, maybe I can come see that farm of yours," Mom says, quick to change the subject. "Honey said it was lovely."

23.

"Honey…" Rosie clamps her hand over her mouth to contain her gasp. "Oh my god!" Recognition sweeps across her face.

"*No*." I burrow my head in my hands. "Mom, oh my god."

"You're Honey Latte, aren't you?"

"What?" Clara clearly has no idea what we're talking about.

Rosie pulls out her phone and swipes through her apps. She's a *fan.* Oh my god. I can see it in the way her eyes light up. Was she pretending not to recognize me this whole time?

"This is going to sound crazy," she says, her eyes on her screen. "But I'm pretty sure…"

The internet is too far-reaching.

I'm glad Rosie and I had a chance to become friends for real before this moment, but God, it's exactly what I've been afraid of.

"Oh wait, you're right!" Clara exclaims, looking over Rosie's shoulder. She turns her screen toward me, and I find myself staring at a picture of Gideon the Goat.

I have no idea what's going on.

"You follow our goat!"

"Yeah! You're one of the top commenters."

"You're Gideon the goat's … *moms*?"

"Uh-huh!" Rosie smiles proudly. "I liked all of your artsy photography posts, so I followed you back."

Mom perks up. "Is this the goat you called and told me about?"

"Mom, *no*," I whisper under my breath.

"She was like, 'Oh my gosh, Mom, @ GideonTheGoat followed me back!' and I couldn't understand what the fuss was about." She takes a long sip of her drink. "Super cute goat, though."

I am going to crawl under the floorboards and stay there until I rot. This explains why their farmhouse looked familiar. When Gideon the goat was a baby, it was the backdrop for a ton of his most popular photos. Dressed in cute jammies, Gideon hopped around on the furniture, making cute sounds. Ugh, my heart is exploding just thinking about it. I graced the same space as my favorite internet celebrity and didn't even know it

"I cannot believe this!" I burrow my head in my hands. I could have met him during our last visit, but I was so worried about getting home to Moth. Now I'm not so sure I made the right choice.

We continue talking about the internet, life, and everything in between, working until the sun is low. Then, we spread out on the porch eating chili from oversized mugs, along with thick slices of cornbread that Clara made. Today has been just the distraction I needed

Rosie and Clara tell me about their experience online: the trolls, the fanart, the self-proclaimed goat experts telling them they're doing everything wrong. With every story, I realize they understand better than I could have imagined. It makes me wonder—if I had bothered to open up to my influencer friends back home, would I even have ended up moving? Maybe there was a community there that I totally ignored, right under my nose.

As the resident elder influencer, Mom chimes in every once in a while. Now that I think about it, she's never had a hard time finding *her people* either. I smile at Clara and Rosie. Even with over a million followers, it took moving to the middle of nowhere to find mine. I feel so ridiculous for assuming they wouldn't understand my problems.

The time for Mom to head to home comes too soon. While Rosie and Clara plant wildflowers in the neat garden plot we created, I help her load her bags into the car. Wrapping my arms around her, I find myself in a hug I don't want to end.

"You know, I really didn't know how to feel about all this," she says lovingly, tucking a strand of hair behind my ear. "But I think you're going to be okay out here."

"I do too," I agree, thankful for her approval. I wish I didn't crave it so much, but we can't fix all our problems in one long weekend.

"Call me, okay? And you're coming home for the holidays—no excuses." As I wave goodbye, sadness pricks at my heart as I watch the iconic "live, laugh, love" sticker fade into the distance. When I round the corner of the cabin and find my new friends, the sadness eases. With or without Moth, I'm going to be just fine.

"Your mom is pretty cool," Clara says.

With how everything has gone the last few days, I'm inclined to agree. I sit on the edge of one of the garden boxes, reaching for a trowel.

"So, you literally grew up online, huh?" Rosie asks, sinking down next to me.

"When I moved out here, I thought I wanted to be done. But I can't just turn it off, you know? Sometimes, it feels like my whole inner monologue is viral sound clips and hashtags."

Clara taps the side of her head. "I think I've replaced half of my math memories with memes I've made about Gideon."

"Long division?" I ask with a dramatic sigh. "Yeah, we don't know her."

"But," Rosie clears her throat as if trying to circle back to my point, "updating the world on the life of our sweet goat son is probably nowhere near as personal as the content you make."

"The first few days I came out here, it felt weird to even set up for breakfast without taking a picture of my coffee mug," I admit. "And like honestly, if I was happy, who cares, right? People can take as many silly pictures of their coffee they want. But…"

"But you weren't happy," Rosie finishes.

I shake my head. I'm tempted to ask if she could see right through my fake laughter in my photos, but I don't dare. "I don't know when it stopped being fun, or if it ever truly was what I wanted, but that doesn't change the fact that there's part of my brain that still wants to create."

I want to capture the way the sun hits my face while I wash dishes in the morning and write a poem that goes underneath the image in an understated italicized font.

23.

I want to document a new recipe in a way that won't be compared to my mom's. Despite bragging to Moth about what a good cook I am, my recipe ideas always tanked. The algorithm decided long ago that beauty and skincare were my thing. Any other venture always lost me followers—but I guess that doesn't matter anymore.

"You have time to figure it out," Rosie says, patting my shoulder. "And you can always just take pictures, you know."

She says it like it's obvious.

I took photos to distract Mom, and to capture lost moments with Moth, but maybe it's time I explore the world with my camera again. This time, for myself.

24.

MOTH IS JUST SCARED. AT LEAST, that's what I tell myself.

He'll come back like last time. I wait for him to darken my doorway and look for him on the rooftop, but days pass, and I don't see one single sign of him. Not even a feather. The forest still sings to me. I hear it when I hike along the trail or work in the garden, but Moth is no longer a part of the song.

He's not in the thicket of trees or the field of flowers. Moth's just … gone. So, I stop looking and waiting. Instead, I create. In just two days, the house has blossomed—literally. I glue pressed flowers to the walls and hang crystals in the windows, nesting and nestling into every crevice of this place. Tulle and lace cover my body as I explore light and shadow in front of the camera. I explore angles and expressions I never would have dared to try before freeing myself from my fake smile.

The last thing I want to see when I open my door is Chris.

He stands on my doorstep with those god-forsaken lattes in one hand and a tool kit in the other. His sheepish grin should make him look handsome, but I know better now. His apple pie face has rotted. It takes everything I have not to recoil when I meet his eyes.

This is the man who ruined everything.

Inviting him in is the last thing I want to do, so I slip outside and take a seat on one of the old rocking chairs on my porch. I could—*should*—tell him to leave, but instead, I accept his company—mostly for the free coffee.

In the morning's quiet moments, the loneliness since Moth left is the worst. I miss too-sweet tea and toast covered in jam. I miss the way Moth's fangs would peek out when he smiled and the surprisingly soft sound of his laugh. So, I do something only fathomable in the deep loneliness. I offer this man, who I've grown to hate, a seat next to me.

"Rosie said your mom went home," Chris says, the chair's rockers squeaking as he rocks.

"Yup."

"She seemed nice."

"She is."

"You've had a lot of house guests lately..." He scans me up and down as if looking for clues. "Is your boyfriend still visiting?"

"He is not my boyfriend.'

"Oh?" Chris visibly perks up as he places one of the to-go mugs in my hands. I take a long sip, basking in the frothy oat milk and floral syrup. Chris may be my least favorite person ever, but damn, does he make a heavenly cup of coffee.

"You like it? This one is a lavender and vanilla syrup." He angles his chair closer; the gleam in his eyes is as sleazy and fake as an apology video.

He wants something.

"Is there a reason for this coffee delivery?" I ask, unable to keep the venom out of my voice.

"Just wanted to check in on that roof of yours." He smiles, seeming unphased by my shift in mood. "Rosie mentioned that you patched it up yourself, and honestly, that tarp looks worse than it sounded."

"Oh, whatever, it's totally fine."

"It is not *like totally* fine," he says in a Valley Girl accent. "At least let me help."

You've seriously done enough, I think.

"It's fine—really," I insist, though my heart isn't in it. Would it be so terrible if I said yes? He owes me for all the trouble he's put me through. I may as well be compensated with labor and lattes. God knows it will cost a fortune when I finally get it properly fixed.

The angry red scars around his neck prove that maybe he's been punished enough.

Chris rises, disappearing behind the house.

"What are you doing?" I call.

"What do you think?"

Could he be any more annoying? When I follow him, I find that he's set up my ladder and is already three rungs into the air. "Can you grab my toolbox?" he asks.

"Get off my roof!'

"I'm not on your roof. I'm on a ladder. Now, will you please grab my toolbox before it gets dark?"

I hate his smug smile. How am I supposed to be mad at him when he's willing to do me such a big favor? And this *coffee*! Ugh, when we first met, I would have swooned. "What's in this for you?"

"Does living in a city seriously make you this cynical?" He raises an eyebrow. "Your beautiful company happens to be enough."

Begrudgingly, I retrieve the toolbox.

"Come on, I'll show you how it's done."

I hate to admit it, but Chris knows what he's doing. It took him no time at all to fix the mess I'd made.

Somehow, he has talked me into making him dinner as a thank you. I don't know how it happened, but we're sitting at my table with a frozen pizza between us.

"Thanks for having me over."

"I'm not sure that I did."

"But I'm here," he takes a bite of pizza, "and you're glad, right?"

"Sure," I offer, unable to give him the answer he wants. I shift in my seat, looking out the window at the tussling leaves; the wind does seem to be picking up.

"I don't like that you're out here alone," he says, taking a long, appraising look around my space. "Not with that thing still on the loose."

"Oh, please." I roll my eyes. Chris doesn't need to know that *thing* was in my bed last week. "I can handle myself."

"Yeah?" Chris takes a long sip of his drink. "I felt a lot safer when your mom—or even L.A. guy—was here with you." He arches an eyebrow.

"You're seriously overthinking it." With a sigh, I push my plate away and rise. "Do you still, um, think someone let it go?"

He stands too, inching closer to me than I would like. Grasping my fingers, he brings them to his neck, where Moth's nails dragged against his skin.

"Probably clawed its way out. These marks are what I get for being reckless. I'm not going to make that same mistake. I need to search the woods again."

So that's what he wanted.

"I'm not letting you run around my property with a gun."

"I'm not asking."

"Too bad."

"Heather—"

"No!"

"Just stay at the farm for a few days until I can catch this thing. I'm so close—people in town are finally starting to listen. I'm going to stuff and mount—"

"Stop!" I shake my hand away from him. "Just stop, okay!"

"Sorry, I know you don't like the whole hunting thing. But that monster—"

"You don't even know him," I interrupt, my face burning with anger.

"Him?"

Shit.

"It," I say hurriedly. "The monster, I mean—"

"Are you fucking with me?" Exasperated, he runs a hand through his sandy blonde hair before laughing. "Oh my god, Heather, you're adorable."

"What?"

"This. This is exactly why you need to stay with me for a few days. If you met a monster, you'd invite them over to drink tea and talk about their feelings."

"That—"

Is an entirely and totally valid assessment of my personality, and I have the heartbreak to prove it.

"It's fine if you don't believe me." Chris shoves his hands in his pockets, looking very much like a sad puppy. "Just think about it, okay? Let me do this for you—for us." He swallows hard.

"I can't." I wish I could scrub the feeling of his hand off my skin. "And there isn't an *us.*"

"We're standing here together, aren't we?" The words are more earnest than I expect. With as strange and sometimes sleazy as Chris has been, it's easy to forget that he's just trying to keep himself and the town safe. Me, included.

He's misguided but not coming from a bad place. Moth did destroy his favorite hangout and maul his neck. Maybe my crush has kept me from thinking clearly.

"You'll call me if you see anything weird, right?"

I stiffly nod. Chris's smile is uneasy, but he seems to believe me for tonight. That's enough.

Figuring out how to get him to call off the angry mob is a problem for tomorrow's Heather.

So, the town knows that Chris caught a "monster."

They also know someone let him go.

Despite what Chris said, after my outburst on hunting, I know I'm still the number one suspect.

Which is fair because the monster is currently back on my roof. I climb the ladder to join him, walking along the shabby roof for the second time today.

He's back in his human form. I'm struck by how vulnerable he appears. My breath catches when our eyes meet. I've been dreaming of this moment, imagining it would be sweeping and romantic like something from a movie. Instead, it feels like he's just walked through the door after a business trip: welcome, wanted, *home.*

"Why are you here?" I ask, claiming the space next to him.

"I could not stay away." His clawed hand reaches for me, but he hesitates. A feeling burns inside me like the stubborn embers of a fire. Moth is the smoke in my lungs.

"I understand you requested I not retur—"

"I'm glad you're here," I say, too eager—desperate even. I bite my bottom lip to keep any more confessions from slipping out.

Moth stiffens, his Adam's apple bobbing. He doesn't want me. He told me as much, and yet the spark remains.

"You're a jerk," I grumble, allowing myself to fall against his chest. His welcoming arms encircle my waist. "I've been so worried about you..."

"The hunter was here."

"You're not allowed to do that," I snap, pulling away just enough to meet his gaze. "You can't tell me we're over, then show up acting jealous. Why are you still watching me? Aren't there any other unsuspecting humans in the woods you can make out with?"

"There is only you." He says it like I'm the only person in the world he's ever loved—maybe I am. But it doesn't give him the right to string me along.

"Do you love me?"

"Is that not apparent?" he snaps. I've never seen him look this flustered. His large hands ball into tight fists at his side. "To love you is truly terrifying."

"Since when do you let fear keep you from what you want?"

"Since the price is your safety."

"Stop, okay?" I shout, crossing my arms. "Stop pretending I'm something—someone—to you. I'm not going to sit here and listen to you tell me that you're some big bad monster and then watch you leave me again."

He graciously does not point out that I'm the one who keeps sending him away.

"There are things you don't understand." Though our thighs touch, he seems so very far away.

"Tell me." I smooth a hair away from his eyes like he's just a man. To me, he is, and maybe that's part of the problem.

"I … cannot."

I grit my teeth, trying to resist the heat growing between our bodies. He's so close, yet so far away. I cup his jaw, turning him to face me. His sullen eyes are yearning.

"Kiss me until you forget," I whisper.

I don't need to tell him twice; he presses me back against the shingles. His wings open like a brilliant canopy above me. The pale moon shines through them like a paper lantern. When his lips find mine, they're not gentle. This is what we are to each other: kisses in the dark and secrets to keep. Tonight, I'll cling to every second. If that's all I can have—just one more night—I'll be happy.

Moth's body shifts off mine. He lifts me tenderly, cradling me against his chest. The hands that had been roughly tugging at the hair at the nape of my neck now wipe tears from my cheek.

When did I start crying?

I shouldn't be surprised that Moth noticed before I did. I wish he hadn't. I wish I had just a few more moments where I didn't know my own feelings and could enjoy the bliss of his touch, the grip of those hands. But I don't just want Moth's body. I want all of him, and just one more night will never be enough.

"Have I hurt you?" he asks, carefully stroking my cheek. I shake my head "no" before he wastes any more time worrying. Physically, I'm fine; it's my heart that's aching.

"I can't do this." I shake my head. "I thought maybe—because God, do I want you, but no—not if this is all we're going to be. You have to tell me what's going on."

He bites his bottom lip, averting those ruby eyes skyward. Finally, he looks back at me. "I fear I might not be who you think I am."

"What are you talking about?"

"Heather—" He clasps my hands tightly in his. "I remember."

25.

FINDING OUT MOTH IS ROYALTY FROM another realm shouldn't be too much of a surprise. He has the vocabulary and attitude of a prince. We sit under the stars, and I listen while he tells me what he remembers—which admittedly, isn't much:

A mother with eyes the color of moss who hummed old songs while she worked in the garden.

A throne room of twisted oak trees and stained glass.

Goblets of wine that sparkle in the sun.

Dancing from sunrise to sunset.

And his exile, though the circumstances are still a mystery.

"Look, I'm no stranger to getting canceled, but being banished from an entire realm is like *so harsh*. You seriously have no idea what you did?"

25.

"You are accepting all of this rather quickly."

I've already had to accept the impossible, it would be unwise to question Moth's origins. It would also be exhausting. It makes sense that he's royalty rather than some feral government experiment. It explains the powers too. Science can do a lot, but I don't think it can make you talk to birds or shapeshift.

"Well yeah, what I don't understand is why are these memories coming back now?" I ask, "When did all of this start, or have you always known?"

"I have had glimpses during our time together, but only in the time we've been apart have the memories become clear."

"Why now?" I ask. He simply shrugs in response appearing to know no more than I do.

I'm holding a prince from another world in my arms. It all seems too good to be true, which begs the question. "Will you have to go back?"

Silence.

I bite my bottom lip to keep it from quivering. Moth has already seen me at my absolute weakest. I don't want him to have to comfort me while I cry *again*.

But the silence stretches out until it is made perfectly clear that I will lose him again. His fingers twine in my hair, and despite the building tension, I allow myself to relax into the feeling of his claws on my scalp.

"Is that what you desire?" His voice is dark, but his fingers continue their gentle ministrations until they reach the back of my neck. "After everything I've done—to be a world away from you?"

"Everything you've done?" I echo. I think of laughing together in a field of flowers. The way he looked bathed in candlelight that night he made us dinner. The kisses, the cuddles, his silly smile. "Why would I want that?"

"Then why, my flame, would I leave?" He leans in close so that his sharp nose is resting on my forehead.

"To be around people like you, to rule over a kingdom, to finally get away from all the—"

His lips silence any argument I have. As he kisses me, each counterpoint melts away.

He breaks away with a sharp gasp.

I didn't think it was possible for him to care about me as much as I care about him. But here we are, woven together like silk and cotton on the roof of my—our—cabin. I can't think of anything more perfect than the two of us under the stars.

But I have roots to this world. He's got to have someone who's missing him, whether friends or family. Now that he has some of his memories back, is it really okay for him to give all that up just for me?

"Heather..."

"Could you come back?" I force the words out before I lose my nerve. "If you left, I mean..."

"I do not know." His arms tighten around my body. Closing my eyes, I breathe in the scent of oak and cinnamon, memorizing the way our bodies fit together. There are so many things that could tear us apart. I never imagined a whole other world would be one of them. We have enough problems here as it is.

"I imagine I committed a grave misdeed to end up in this realm."

"Okay." I nod.

"Oh…kay?" As I slide my hand back into his, he stares at me with those unblinking, bewildered eyes.

"Whatever it is…" I lean my shoulder against him, letting out a yawn. "I like the person in front of me, even if your past is a part of that. We'll figure it out."

"It is not that simple."

"Why?" I ask, cupping his face in my hands. He averts his eyes momentarily before meeting my determined gaze. "You don't even know what you did. Why let it stop you from being happy? Besides, if it's the reason you ended up here. I'm *glad* you did it—whatever it is."

"You—" He hesitates. "You have no idea what you might be accepting."

"I'm accepting you," I say with a deep breath. "Even if you are like a murderous traitor or something."

"I beg you to have higher standards."

"I'd rather have you." I plant a kiss on his cheek and savor the way his pale skin turns a rosy shade of pink.

"I have nothing to offer you," he says weakly, his eyes already dark with desire. There's a familiar bulge straining against the sheath that protects his modesty. We've fumbled in the dark together so many times, I've never gotten a good look at the exoskeleton that gives him the illusion of pants. My fingers leisurely trail across his growing hardness. I enjoy the feeling of him coming to life under my touch.

"I mean I wouldn't call that nothing," I tease, planting my lips on his. His guttural moan makes my lips vibrate.

"I've been thinking about you too," I say, not so subtly letting the fabric of my nightgown fall away from my shoulder.

"*Here?*" he asks, a dark brow raising with interest.

"They're our woods, right?" I whisper, laying his body down upon the roof; I straddle his thick waist. "Let's play a game. You're not allowed to touch me until I say so." He stiffens but nods in agreement.

The way he's looking up at me suddenly makes me feel bashful, but I don't let myself cower under his gaze. I want him to see all of me.

"You are so beautiful," he murmurs. His hands twitch, but he doesn't move.

"Good job," I whisper, letting my nightgown spill across his body. The soft layers of chiffon trail down his bare chest. His strong jaw clenches with the light touch of the fabric.

He closes his eyes. I wonder if he'll break before I do. The longing I have for him to lunge for me and end the game before it begins grows, but I stay strong. I'm not done tormenting him yet.

"Do you want me?" I whisper. His throat bobs in response.

"Moth…?" Sinking down until my mouth has found his neck, I purse my lips as if to plant a gentle kiss. Instead, I bite with all the force I can muster.

He gasps, growing even harder beneath me. Oh, this is fun. A smirk plays across my lips.

Tonight, I'm going to make him melt.

The look in his half-lidded eyes is almost pained, dizzy with desire. When he reaches for me, I pin his hands down at his sides and kiss him with every ounce of longing I've saved up since he's kept himself away from me.

"I missed you so much," I say, holding tight to both of his hands. My lips brush against his jaw, then neck, until my kisses trail lazily down his chest.

"Heather."

"Hmm?" I plant a kiss on his abdomen, working my way down to the spot just under his navel; when I reach his hip, I take the tender skin between my teeth and bite.

"*Please*." The breathy desperation in his voice is delicious.

"Do you want me to stop?" I ask.

"No, but you … you do not have to."

"I don't *have to* do anything." I find my way to his other hip. This time, I bite hard, kissing and sucking at his flesh, reveling in each sweet moan.

We're more similar than I thought.

"Tell me if you want me to stop."

"I *want* to touch you."

"Aww, that's too bad." I rest across his body for a few moments. Then finally I kiss across his skin until I'm at the center of Moth's hips. My fingers graze down the length of his impressive shaft, and although he still doesn't move, I feel him bucking beneath me. I hadn't noticed the way the gold flecks that cover his skin reach all the way down here. I connect each sparkling freckle with my tongue.

Let the record show that as far as penises go, *Mothman* has a pretty good one. I've seen some art online that would suggest that he has a subsection of fans who would be very jealous of me in this moment.

Cryptid, monster, prince from another realm.

The old titles and rumors melt away with each gasp I pry from his lips.

There are so many ways I could tease him. For a moment, I don't touch him, my hot breath dampening his skin. Then, I try to take his entire length into my mouth. Considering his size, I'm not even sure that I manage to get halfway down his shaft. Still, it feels like we are made specially for each other. I work my mouth down until he hits the back of my throat. Moth moans, clenching the roof tiles with his claws. My work has had the desired effect.

I work my mouth up and down, trailing my tongue up in a flicking motion. Every moan from his lips spurs me on—I hunger to bring him over the edge.

"Heather." This demon of a man says my name like a prayer, begging for me to release him from my torment. He crushes the roof tiles into powder—I'm definitely going to need another tarp before the next storm. He arches his back, and his wings splay out under us, knocking me a little off balance. I steady myself.

"I need you," he growls.

"Good," I whisper back, letting go of his hands. Moth reclaims his freedom by grasping at my waist and poising to thrust inside me. A giggle escapes me as I crash back down onto his hips. It's all happening hard and fast and *exactly* how I imagined.

His features morph like liquid into both monster and man. The bones of his body crack and shift as his claws sharpen to rake down my back. As he shifts, Moth's movements come harder and faster than ever before. I match him thrust for thrust until waves of pleasure drag me into their depths. I'm drowning in his touch.

The monster who chased me through the woods is fucking me on this roof—and I've never been more in love. When I try to kiss him, he pulls his face away, making me heave a frustrated sigh.

"You would kiss this face?" he asks, capturing my chin with the tip of his claws. His owlish eyes soften into two red puddles.

"Over and over and over," I whisper in his ear. He allows me to lean forward. His beak-like mouth is hard on mine, but I don't let the shape stop me from exploring the ways we fit together. I'm finding it fun to wrap my mouth around the whole thing like it's the bottom of an ice cream cone and letting my tongue do the rest. By the way his body responds, I *know* he likes it too. This man—this monster—is all mine.

He keeps me riding the edge of my impending orgasm. Pinning my arms behind my back, the momentary denial threatens to pull me under.

When his pace quickens, I unravel, writhing, weak, and breathless in his arms. He meets me there just moments later, pulling me close as his body fills mine.

"If this is what make up sex looks like, the two of us should fight, like all the time," I joke.

He growls in my ear, and I tremble, savoring the feeling of being tucked in his arms again.

"You will be the death of me," he says.

"Oh, you love it."

"I *love* you." His large eyes soften the harsh line of his monstrous face. Even the beak is cute, once you get used to it. At the moment he's owl-ish and almost shy-looking.

"I love you too." I plant a kiss on his cheek before snuggling closer. "There is still something I don't understand."

"If there's just one single thing, I would say you are doing better than I."

"If you could heal yourself this whole time, why did you stay so long at my place?"

"My body would not allow it."

"What do you mean?"

"To use my energy to create somewhere safe to heal. Try as I might, it would not allow it. I'm not a believer in magic. But I thought, perhaps, you had bewitched me."

Hence why he asked if I was a witch when we first met...

"And now?"

"Now, I am certain."

"I'm just a normal girl."

"And that is enough." His beak is firm when it touches my lips in a small peck. *Enough.* I've never been enough, not in my whole life. I've always needed to do more, be more—funnier, fitter, trendier. It's part of the reason that all I wanted when I moved out here was to disappear.

I don't think I want that anymore.

His palm runs across the roof. "This place. You've made me safe, taken care me even when I didn't deserve it. You welcomed me into your cocoon." He wraps me in his arms, and the feathers on his neck brush against my forehead.

25.

"Maybe you should lay low for a few days." It pains me just to suggest it. I don't want to untangle our bodies ever again. "Those assholes are planning on looking for you all weekend. I told them not to come here, but Chris just keeps showing up. I feel like he knows something…" I bite my bottom lip. Those hunters hurt Moth—badly.

I can't risk losing him.

"You are pushing me away *again*." He sounds somewhat annoyed, as if being away from me for a few days will be a horrible inconvenience. I'm glad he knows it isn't personal.

"I just need you to be safe. I feel like they might poke around again. I don't want to think about what they'll do if they find you." I exhale, snuggling closer.

"Or what they will do to the human who harbored the monster." His arms tighten possessively

"Please, *I'll* be fine." Someone needs to stick around to throw these guys off Moth's trail, and if I'm here, I can hopefully use some of my PR skills to get a handle on this situation. With the way Chris has just been showing up at the cabin, there's no way Moth can be here, even in his human form. It's too risky. I'll fix all of this and get us a clean slate.

Relief pours through me when he finally nods.

"If it will give you peace of mind." His antennae fluff in the breeze. "I can stay outside of these woods, but only until their hunt is over. When the sun rises on Monday, I will be home in your arms."

I pepper soft kisses across his skin, smiling against him. "And then we'll be inseparable, I promise."

"I will hold you to that."

"Thank you."

"But you must promise me you'll also *'lay low.'* Do not seek out this Chris." He sits up, cradling me in his arms like I'm the most precious thing in the world. "And do not let him into our home."

Our home. He says the words without even realizing it. I've though the same, but hearing it from his lips is different.

"I promise." No one is looking for me. He's the one who's in danger. I could go with him, but where? No, I'll sort this out first. Like any scandal, we just need to wait a few days and it will all blow over.

Moth scoops me in his arms and lowers me to the porch before flying off to safety. I watch him go, a pang of sadness spreading through my chest.

It must be absolutely gorgeous to have wings like that; seeing him soar through the sky makes me wish I could follow him. The rest of the evening is spent stress-snacking on a bag of paleo-puffs and sulking in bed.

I literally *just* got him back.

What was I thinking sending him away again? Pulling myself out of bed, I pad across the wooden floors to retrieve a glass of water.

Relief crashes through me like a wave when I hear the door. Moth's footsteps echo behind me. A smirk pulls at my lips. I should have known he wouldn't be able to leave my firelight for too long.

"You really couldn't stay away, could you?" I can't keep the flirtation out of my voice. I should be upset he didn't listen to my warning. Instead, I'm relieved. Yes, we made a plan, but we can figure out how to deal with the hunters together. I squint in the dark, but Moth's red eyes are not staring back at me.

"I'm really sorry about this." Chris's voice is eerily calm. He steps toward me, a coarse rope in his hands.

"Get out of my house," I hiss, pulling open the drawer and grabbing a knife. It's pink and green and designed to cut watermelon. It does absolutely nothing to intimidate him.

"Heather, I'm doing this for you," he soothes. "You're a sweet girl, and you don't know what you're messing with."

"Get. Out. Of. My. House." The knife quakes in my grip.

"You're being ridiculous." He laughs. "The door was open. I just wanted to make sure you were okay."

I loosen my grip on the handle. It wouldn't be the first time I'd forgotten to lock a door. But if that were true, he wouldn't have that look in his eyes; he wouldn't be holding a rope in his hands. "Put down the knife, Heather."

"You need to leave."

"Just tell me where the monster is, and this won't get ugly..."

"I don't know what you're talking about."

He reaches into his pocket and pulls out a scrap of fabric. I recognize it from the shirt Moth accidentally tore when we were in the bed of Chris's truck. "Does this look familiar?"

Shit shit shit.

He lunges forward, easily knocking the knife from my grasp. It clatters across the floor.

"HELP!" The fear in my voice is unrecognizable. If Moth listened to me, he's long gone, but that doesn't mean someone isn't out there who might hear me. I thrash against Chris, kicking and screaming. Finally, I break free only to feel the rope looped around my wrists.

"I'm not going to hurt you." He hauls me out toward his truck. I dig my heels in the ground.

"Then don't fucking kidnap me!" Tears bubble up in my eyes as he throws me in the backseat. Chris doesn't even have the decency to tell me what he wants, but I'm sure it has something to do with Moth.

I hate that it's all happened so fast.

I hate that I couldn't defend myself.

I hate that Mom was right. I shouldn't have been out here by myself.

Oh, Moth...

He told me to be safe. He made me *promise.* I will find my way back to the cabin—our new life depends on it.

THE IDEA THAT I COULD ESCAPE WAS CUTE. Really adorable that I thought I could get away from Chris with his detailed plan and his very thick rope. He's taken me to his crumbling clubhouse, the eaves cloaked in shadow. Every breath I take is thick with sawdust. My lungs already ache from the stale air—and my screams.

I've fought and kicked and pleaded, but it's no use. I can't get away. I rock back and forth in the chair. Whether it's been minutes or hours is a mystery. My skin is raw from the rough rope that binds me. Chris has "sincerely apologized" for "having" to use me as bait, so there's that.

He comes and goes until the barn is riddled with traps. I rock harder; finally, the chair tips forward and

I crawl toward the door. In the dark, I bump into the wall, and news clippings rain down like confetti.

"Would you just sit still?" Chris snaps, turning back toward me. "Please, it's dangerous." He gestures at a metal contraption a few feet from me. My gut sinks. I nearly crawled straight into a bear trap.

We've been playing this game for hours, and he's losing patience with me. The gentle apple-pie faced guy I met my first day in town disappears with each feeble attempt to escape.

Moth isn't a monster; he's never been. If Chris would just listen to me, he'd see that. But why look for truth when blood is so much more satisfying? Chris can almost taste his revenge. I'm the meat on the hook that will finally give him Moth's head mounted on the wall.

Fear crawls up my throat, squeezing until my mouth is dry. Angry tears burn my eyes. I've tried so hard not to cry, but these ropes are killing me.

"Hey, hey, hey," Chris gasps, kneeling next to me. He brings a cup of water to my lips, and despite the urge to spit it back in his face, I drink. I'm just so tired. "You just have to wait a little longer. I'm sorry it's come to this, but it will be over soon, I promise. Whatever spell he has you under will break as soon as he's dead."

"I told you, it's not like that!" I shout. I try to, at least, but my voice cracks with each word. Chris tilts my chin and wipes my tears away while I tremble. "Don't!" Every part of his skin that touches mine is a violation.

"Shhhh," he coos in my ear. "That thing tricked you." He moves away, and I notice, for the first time, the gun in his hands. "But I'm going to take care of everything, okay? The monster somehow forced you to let it go—to hide it from me, but it won't be able to hurt you anymore. After tonight, you'll see."

I shake my head. I don't want to let this man see me cry, but the hysterics start nonetheless. "He's never hurt me—he's not going to hurt anyone!"

"It chased my friends and I down like animals. It would eat us alive if it had the chance. You … you've been claimed or something. It has some sort of connection to you."

"What? No, that's not—"

"A mind-control spell, maybe. I know the ropes are uncomfortable, but I can't have you running back to it. Can it sense where you are? Is it leeching your energy?"

"Chris, I told you. That isn't how that works. He's not what you think."

"I've done enough research into the paranormal to know when something is … wrong. I'm not going to let it hurt you anymore, okay?" Chris frowns, brushing a stray hair away from my tear-streaked face. "If you are connected, can he feel what's happening to you right now?"

"You're not making any sense."

"Does the monster know where you are?"

"Of course not! If he did, he would be here! Moth lov—" I bite my bottom lip. I didn't mean—oh god. I can see him piecing together what I almost said. *He knows.* His eyes narrow.

"You're more than just protecting him, *aren't you*?"

"I—"

"Heather, this is serious." Chris's eyes skew with pure hatred, but he sounds eerily calm. "If that

sentence was going where I think it was, we're going to have a problem. I need to draw him out—"

He wraps the ropes around me more tightly, and the dull pain twists into my bones until I scream.

"I—" I can't do this. My body involuntarily shakes as I choke on my own breath, sucking in air, unable to swallow. He has a gun. Chris has a gun, and the more I look at it, the more I fall apart.

"Heather, I'm sorry. I didn't mean—" He fumbles, bending down next to me. His voice is tender again, like a fairy tale prince. "I'm just trying to summon him or something. If you two are connected in the way I think you are, then he should know you're in danger."

"Am I?"

He pauses, as if hearing himself for the first time. "No, I mean … you know I'm not going to hurt you. I would never."

"That is *literally* all you are doing!"

I wonder if he still sees himself as the hero.

Heroes don't kidnap people.

Heroes don't tie people to chairs.

Heroes don't—God—If Moth falls into these traps, how much could he survive? I need to try to snap Chris out of this. I've tried force, reason, truth, and in my desperation, I'm not above begging.

"Please, please, just stop all of this, okay? It's not too late. Think about how pissed Rosie and Clara will be that you kidnapped their new best friend."

"Shit…" He gasps, bending down to look into my eyes. "You left out some details in that little story of yours, didn't you? When I saw him flying above your cabin, I knew something was happening, but I never thought. You really—you and that thing?"

"I love him, Chris, and he loves me." I plead. "He's not who you think he is."

"Monster fucker." His mouth twitches with disgust. I hate how pathetic I must look in this moment, but this moment of clarity is the closest I've gotten to getting through to him. "You're not even under any kind of spell, *are you*?" Chris's voice cracks.

Before I can shake my head, he grabs the back of the chair and drags me to the center of the room.

"Oh, *come on*!" I groan. "Do you not get it? If he finds me like this, he's going to kill you."

"I'd like to see it try." Chris smugly tosses his handgun from one hand to the other as if this is all some sort of game.

"Death would be mercy." In a blur of shadow and feather, Moth dives from the rafters with his claws poised at Chris's neck. This time, I'm not sure if I should stop him.

"*Moth.*" His name falls out of my mouth, and he gives me a steady look that says, 'I'm here now. Everything is going to be okay.' His owl eyes are soft and round, and I itch to feel safe in his arms again.

It's just a moment, but it's all Chris needs to fire.

27.

MOTH IS UNHURT.

With a swipe of his claws, I'm unbound from the chair and safe in his arms. Chris was tossed aside like a ragdoll, but I think I can see the rising and falling of his chest. So, that's good. I'd say getting out of a situation like this without anyone dying is a 10/10.

I smile up at Moth.

He found me.

Of course, he found me.

I'm his person—his flame.

We are always going to be weirdly drawn together.

But when he stares at me, his eyes are hollow. He focuses on my lower body—the marks from the rope, I guess. Except, when I follow his eyes, I discover that the periwinkle fabric of my nightgown is stained red.

27.

No.

With shaking hands, I touch the damp stain.

Is that blood?

No.

It couldn't have hit me.

If it did, I wouldn't be—

My legs give way from under me. Moth cradles me in his arms. He's shaking. My blood stains his hands the color of merlot.

"Heather." He says my name, but I can't hear it right. My body is falling away from this bloodstained barn. My name plays over and over like a song on the radio.

Heather, Heather, Heather...

It plays from the old radio our hipster neighbors had in that apartment Mom and I lived in during high school. I lay on the bed in my pastel bedroom, the song echoing like a dream.

The walls are light purple.

Moth is staring at me from the painted white doorway. He seems further and further away with every passing breath.

I open my eyes, and I can't remember where I am. I know there are arms around me. I can't feel them, but I know he's still here.

Home. He feels like home, but Moth is an old photo fading at the edges. There's comfort and nostalgia and pain. The world tilts, hazy and black. Moth always did look good in shadow. I think I can see his red eyes looking back at me—they are unusually dim.

His forehead presses so tight against mine it should hurt, but I can't feel it. I can't feel him at all—I'm a ghost in his arms.

"You are alright." His usually measured voice is panicked and breathy. "You *will be* alright."

If someone like him is scared, then I'm as good as dead. I can tell by the quake of his fingertips fading against my skin.

I realize it all at once. There's no light to draw me close. No highlight reel of the life I've lived. Just the thought: *I'm going to die.* Over and over again.

Darkness pulls me into a tight cocoon. I feel it wrap around me, layer by layer.

"I'm glad I got to save you one last time." The words come out as a whisper. I clutch onto his hand, unsure if they made it to his ears.

Sometimes, death means new beginnings

Tonight, it means goodbye.

I'M ALIVE?

Or dreaming. It's hard to be sure. With a sharp intake of breath, I'm soothed by the scent of oak. Moth's body is holding tight to mine, which means wherever I am, it's safe. The air is so thick I can almost taste it, but it's void of the grainy sawdust of the barn.

"You are awake," he gasps, extending a claw to stroke the flesh of my cheek. Warmth pours through my core.

I never thought I'd see him again. Our bodies are entangled in this dark space as if we're zipped together in a sleeping bag—huh. I'm reminded of the cocoon I found Moth in the night he was captured. Is it possible he encased us both in something like that?

"Where are we?" I whisper, blinking the world into existence.

"Safe, my flame." If that's true, then why does he sound so mournful?

Light chips away at our surroundings, and I realize that we *are* inside some kind of cocoon, I touch the walls, cringing at the warm sticky texture. The structure cracks open before either of us are braced for it, revealing our hiding place far up in the trees.

Not expecting to be launched into open air, I stumble away from Moth, and though he lunges for me, the speed of my fall evades his grasp completely.

Once again, I'm plummeting to my doom. I don't feel Moth's arms snatch around my waist, but he must because suddenly I'm weightless over the edge of the ground where a pile of leaves meet a crystal-clear stream.

"You saved me again." I exhale. My bare feet touch the leaves and I lean back into his arms. I try to, at least. I stumble, looking up toward the tree I'd fallen from.

"My flame…"

Moth hangs in the sky, a furrow to his brow. If he didn't catch me, then how did I get down here? I walk to the edge of the stream. In the water, a strange reflection stares back at me. It's like I'm looking at myself through a filter designed to put Moth's features on my body. My wings are delicate black and light green silk spread wide across my back, and two feathery antennae dance in the wind on the top of my head.

This has to be someone else, but the reflection reaches up to touch her face at the same time I touch mine. My jaw goes slack, as does hers. How is this possible?

28.

"This ... this is me?" My antennae bobble as I poke them with my fingers. They're wide and fluffy and cuter than anything I could have dreamt up for myself.

"I am sorry..." Moth whispers from the sky. He lingers there as if he's afraid to get too close.

"Why? Holy shit this is amazing!" I say, before clasping my hand over my mouth, but I can't help it. Not only am I alive, but I just got, like ten times hotter.

"Sorry, I uh..." I open my light green wings, marveling at how natural this all feels.

Moth tilts his head, gracefully landing next to me. His fingers tuck under my chin, lifting my gaze to his.

"That was not the reaction I expected." His smile is bright with relief, but it doesn't ease the worry from his tender gaze. "You are not angry?"

I can't understand why he looks so sad.

"I'm not." I grasp his hands tightly. A smile makes its way across my face. I lean my head on his chest. He's been alone in these woods for so long.

"We should talk about what has happened..."

"*After* we kiss?" I ask, stretching my new wings, fluttering up off the ground until I meet his lips. He holds me by the waist and nods.

"Who am I to argue with you?" He launches us upward; above the treetops, we soar and kiss until last night feels like a bad dream.

"I was not ready to lose you." He presses his forehead to mine, breathing in the scent of my hair.

"I wasn't ready to go," I admit, relaxing against him. We perch in a tree, just like the one I fell out of today and when we first met. I cup his cheek, gently turning his face to meet mine.

"You will never feel alone again," he whispers in my ear. I melt closer to him.

"And neither will you." Nuzzling into the crook of his shoulder, I let out a small laugh. "Let's haunt these woods together from now on, okay?"

His smile is bright and toothy in response. "I like the sound of that."

Epilogue

One year later.

HOMEMADE CINNAMON ROLLS.

Two cups of tea, both sweetened with honey with rose petals dancing on top.

I hover over the table, trying to get the perfect shot. I want to capture the way the light is flowing through the window. The Polaroid camera snaps and flashes, and the picture pops out of the slot. I set it down on the patched-up lace tablecloth and watch it develop while Moth takes a bite of his cinnamon roll.

One photo a day of something—anything I want, but namely the things that make me happy.

I'm still figuring out what those things are, but this is undeniable.

Moth holds a piece of the cinnamon roll out to me with clawed hands.

The bliss of this morning can't be contained to one picture.

Sometimes, I share these moments with the world—it depends on how I'm feeling.

People were split when I came back to my accounts, but the messages of support and concern are the ones I try to focus on.

I want to start sharing my art, writing, and photography again. But only the projects that light the spark in my soul I'm still working on getting back.

Moth's eyes glint red above the rim of his teacup.

Some things are just for my eyes, and I'm okay with that.

I'm not done finding myself yet. But it's nice to be on this journey with someone who is even more camera shy than I am.

"Have I told you of your beauty this morning?" he asks, his lips on my fingertips, kissing every piece of skin that's caked in icing.

"You may have mentioned it." Although I try to be coy, we've been together for a year. He knows just what to say to make my heart race. "Rosie and Clara are coming over later so do not—I repeat, *do not*—eat all the cinnamon rolls."

He glares but says nothing. A year ago, he would complain about crowding the house with humans, but he likes Rosie and Clara. They like him too.

Sure, it was a little awkward explaining the whole "Surprise, I'm dating the monster your brother has been hunting, and also he kind of shot me, and now I'm *also* a moth-creature-person, but I hope we can still be friends" thing. Still, after a few dozen lengthy conversations, we got there. And Chris is getting the help he needs with some serious counseling.

Maybe one day he could earn my forgiveness, but I doubt it. Besides, Moth would tear his throat out if he so much as looked in my direction. Weirdly, I think that might be something I love about him.

"The humans will be coming over in an hour?" Despite the cold words, I detect a hint of fondness in his voice.

"*Rosie and Clara* will be over at 11."

"It seems we have enough time for a walk." He stands, offering me his arm, which I gladly take. We follow the familiar path down to the lake. We usually save our flying for the evening, traveling as far as our wings will take us. With a few cleverly placed hats and tinted sunglasses, we've gone a little farther than our backyard. I can shift back to look fully human if I need to, but Moth's wings are always a part of him. Just like some of my "human-ness" hasn't left me. I still take thyroid medication every morning and was eternally grateful when nothing strange came up on my recent bloodwork. Moth didn't so much as bring me back to life as he did heal my wounds. There's still human blood in my veins, despite the more interesting recent developments.

In the privacy of our woods, I let my wings span out behind me as we walk. Moth was surprised at how quickly I picked up flying. It's given me freedom I could have only ever dreamed of before. We've soared over beaches and different cities. We even spent the holiday season down in Florida. My mom spent the entire visit begging me to share my new skincare routine. She thinks the mountain air has been doing me a lot of favors. She adores Moth too. I've kept all the other details from her, but maybe, one day, I'll tell her everything like I used to.

Moth and I have found comfort in the shadows while still managing to step out of them together. However, days like this are still my favorites. This place is home, and for all the "strange things" I was warned about in these woods, I'm glad we found each other. Lately, though, things have felt surprisingly ordinary. For two moth-creatures living in the woods, we've made a quiet little life together, and I couldn't be happier.

As we walk, I notice an odd gleam from the hollow of a nearby oak tree.

"Hey, do you see that?" I pull on Moth's arm until we're both staring at the light. It's gold and has an almost liquid sheen to it. I'm tempted to reach in and touch it, but my fingers pause in mid-air when an object flies *through* the tree, as though it's a portal.

The prismatic light dims, and on the forest floor rests a scroll of old-looking parchment.

Moth retrieves it, his eyes darting across the words on the glowing parchment. His lips press in a straight line—it's all less than reassuring.

"We have been summoned." Moth sighs, drawing me close. His chin rests on the top of my head. The space around our bodies glows the same shade of gold as the letter. I don't know where we're going, but I think our visit with Rosie and Clara is going to have to wait. Our quiet slice of life in the woods seems like it's about to get a whole lot less ordinary. I hold tight to Moth's hand knowing that whatever comes next, we'll be in it together.

Heather and Moth will return in
I'm Engaged to Mothman. Stay tuned for
a meet the parents you won't forget.

ACKNOWLEDGEMENTS

A GIANT THANK YOU TO MY HUSBAND Matt who encouraged me to escape into this fictional world (and has not once judged me for my giant cryptid crush). Thank you for always listening to my ideas, pointing out all my spelling errors, and making sure I drink water and sleep while I'm in the thrall of inspiration. You've shown me how sweet true love is, and that will always be reflected in my work because of you. You're the best partner I could hope for and there's no one I'd rather kiss–including Mothman. :p

Thank you to Taylor Simonds for our car-port coffees, conversations, and for keeping me company even when we had to sit 6-feet apart. You've taught me how to hone my craft as a writer and reach for the stars, and I'm so grateful for all our bookish and vintage adventures.

To all the artists of sexy Mothman fanart–thank you for fueling my creativity and curiosity as my infatuation for this character grew.

A giant thank you to 4 Horsemen Publications for their support of my first-ever adult romance. I've always wanted to write a series and cannot wait to work on books two and three! To my editor Beau Lake, you have been a dream to work with and I am so thankful for your notes and encouragement.

Thank you to Erin Denton and Meaghan Carey for your insight and feedback on so many small elements of this story. You cheered me on, asked the right questions, and have been so incredibly supportive of this story since day one.

And last, but not least, thank you to my spooky sister Lashes Lane for making me laugh, sharing the goofiest memes, and helping me keep imposter syndrome at bay. In the age of the internet, I'm no stranger to burnout, and I'm so grateful I have you to lean on and brainstorm with. Your "Hey, this is really good" messages when I shared snippets of this story with you helped me keep going. Thanks for always taking breaks from being a badass burlesque babe to listen to me talk about Mothman's butt.

BOOK CLUB QUESTIONS

1. What could Heather have done differently to prevent her "internet-burnout" at the start of the book?

2. Living in the digital age, have you ever felt similarly overwhelmed by life online?

3. Heather often refers to being "at home" with Moth. What is it about their dynamic that you believe gives her that feeling?

4. How would the book have played out differently in a different time period or setting?

5. How familiar with Mothman were you before reading this book?

6. Would you kiss Mothman in his non-human form? Did you find his looks cute or creepy?

7. Did you notice the parallels to Beauty and The Beast in this story?

8. Do you feel like Chris deserves a redemption arc?

9. If you had a pair of moth wings, what color would they be?

10. If you could talk to the author, what burning question would you want to ask?

You don't have to just wonder; I'd love to virtually chat with your book club! Send me a Tweet @mrspaigelavoie to chat about all things Moth and Heather or email me at mrspaigelavoie@gmail.com to set up a formal author discussion.

ABOUT THE AUTHOR

PAIGE LAVOIE IS A HALLOWEEN-LOVING cinnamon roll who writes stories about misfits, monsters, and falling in love. Her affection for cozy autumn moments, charming protagonists, and all things cute and creepy is reflected in the worlds she creates. When Paige isn't writing, she can be found hunting for treasures at the local antique mall and sipping oat milk lattes under a lacy parasol as she hides from the sun in her home state of Florida.

More books from 4 Horsemen Publications

Romance

Ann Shepphird
The War Council

Emily Bunney
All or Nothing
All the Way
All Night Long: Novella
All She Needs
Having it All
All at Once
All Together
All for Her

KT Bond
Back to Life
Back to Love
Back at Last

Lynn Chantale
The Baker's Touch
Blind Secrets
Broken Lens
Blind Fury
Time Bomb
VIP's Revenge
Chef's Taste

Mandy Fate
Love Me, Goaltender
Captain of My Heart

Mimi Francis
Private Lives
Private Protection
Private Party
Run Away Home
The Professor
Our Two-Week, One-Night Stand

Shae Coon
Bound in Love
Controlling Assets
For His Own Protection
Her Broken Pieces
The Roma's Claim
The Roma's Promise

Fantasy, SciFi, & Paranormal Romance

Amanda Fasciano
Waking Up Dead
Dead Vessel

Beau Lake
The Beast Beside Me
The Beast Within Me
Taming the Beast: Novella
The Beast After Me
Charming the Beast: Novella
The Beast Like Me
An Eye for Emeralds
Swimming in Sapphires
Pining for Pearls

Chelsea Burton Dunn
By Moonlight

Danielle Orsino
Locked Out of Heaven
Thine Eyes of Mercy
From the Ashes
Kingdom Come
Fire, Ice, Acid, & Heart
A Fae is Done

J.M. Paquette
Klauden's Ring
Solyn's Body
The Inbetween
Hannah's Heart
Call Me Forth
Invite Me In
Keep Me Close

Jessica Salina
Not My Time

Kait Disney-Leugers
Antique Magic

Lyra R. Saenz
Prelude
Falsetto in the Woods: Novella
Ragtime Swing
Sonata
Song of the Sea
The Devil's Trill
Bercuese
To Heal a Songbird
Ghost March
Nocturne

Paige Lavoie
I'm in Love with Mothman

Robert J. Lewis
Shadow Guardian and the Three Bears

T.S. Simons
Antipodes
The Liminal Space
Ouroboros

Caim
Sessrúmnir
The 45th Parallel

Valerie Willis
Cedric: The Demonic Knight
Romasanta: Father of Werewolves
The Oracle: Keeper of the Gaea's Gate

Artemis: Eye of Gaea
King Incubus: A New Reign

V.C. Willis
The Prince's Priest
The Priest's Assassin
The Assassin's Saint

Discover more at 4HorsemenPublications.com

Printed in the USA
CPSIA information can be obtained
at www.ICGtesting.com
LVHW042013291023
762487LV00004B/446